THE WHITE LINE

J. S. HELMS

First printing edition 2026.

ISBN: (eBook) - 978-1-962891-11-0
ISBN: (Paperback) - 978-1-962891-08-0

The White Line

Published by Vellichor and More
www.vellichorandmore.com

THE WHITE LINE

PROLOGUE

THREE YEARS EARLIER

A DELIGHTED SHRIEK split the air as Tyler tripped and logrolled down the grassy slope. At the bottom, Kiki leapt on top of him, her tail pumping furiously back and forth as her tongue bathed Tyler's laughing face. The boy's attempt at keeping his lips together during the onslaught of the slobbery tongue while laughing had Jonas grinning.

Jonas and Kristy watched their son from the picnic table under the shade of a towering maple tree. Kristy collected the dirty paper plates and plastic containers. "Getting Tyler that dog was a great idea, Jonas." She piled everything back into the picnic basket. "They've bonded so quickly."

"Not only that," Jonas nodded toward the pair now running in circles, "but they can wear each other out." He stood and hefted the basket with one arm, wrapping the other around his wife's shoulders. "Win-win." He kissed the top of her head.

Walking to the car, Jonas shielded his eyes from the

blinding sun glare off the lake. "Tyler, Kiki, time to head home!"

The two began to run back toward them, Kiki outpacing Tyler with easy lopes. Kristy stepped forward with Kiki's leash, kneeling down to catch the puppy's wriggling body. The black lab mix had a patch of white on her head that, if you squinted just right, resembled a heart.

Tyler arrived huffing and puffing, grass stuck in his hair, cheeks windblown and sun-pinked. He leaned against his kneeling mother in an exaggerated flop of exhaustion.

Jonas paused, watching them. The sun shone on their smiling faces—happiness, love, and laughter—

ACT I

CHAPTER ONE

EARLY MORNING SUN, twirling dust motes trapped in its stream of light, slanted through the window.

Each new day was easier.

Each new day was harder.

Jonas sat at his desk, scrolling down the list of emails in his inbox. His second-hand desk, scratched and gouged from decades of use, held his laptop—shiny tech with blinking lights. At one corner sat a framed portrait of himself, Kristy, Tyler, and their dog Kiki smiling by the rose bushes in their backyard. It faced him while he worked. He would catch himself stepping into that photo to feel closer to his family on rough days. At the other corner, a stack of paperwork waited to be acknowledged. The rest of the scarred desk's work surface was bare, controlled.

He focused on the inbox, the glare of the screen at odds with the soft, morning sunlight. Spam, spam, electric bill, spam, Donna Lightner. He stopped scrolling, and clicked his mouse to open the email from his sister-in-law.

Hi Jonas!

It's been a while since we've talked. I hope you are doing okay. You know you can always ask if you need anything.

The reason I'm messaging you is about Phil. He's graduating this year—can you believe it?? And he specifically asked me to ask you if you'd come to his graduation. It would mean a lot for his Uncle Jonas to be there. It's been such a rough road, but he's made it!

Anyway, I'm sorry I'm not giving you very much notice. Graduation is next Friday. And you are welcome to stay with us. Let me know!

Love,
Donna

Jonas sighed and leaned back in his chair. Outside his office window, the world was waking up. A group of teens walked by, bouncing on their toes. Laughing, they pushed and shoved each other. They were about the same age as Phil.

He really couldn't manage a few days off. Folding his hands together over his stomach, he stared unseeing across his office. Renovations, upcoming teen tournament, fundraiser, yeah, that just wouldn't work. Grace Street Ministry was a busy place.

Politicians' promises of uplifted living for the downtrodden had mostly collapsed into further destitution. That was Grace Street's neighborhood. Its mission field. The ministry sat in a large, partially renovated brick home. Its

Victorian detailing reflected a more prosperous time in the neighborhood a century prior. Now it looked slightly odd surrounded by much newer, but more dilapidated, subsidized housing.

Jonas, the Pastoral Care Coordinator, was tasked with providing the community with a beacon of hope, unconditional love, and God's grace in an environment of discarded needles on the streets and prostitutes on the corners. The ministry housed a clothing closet, soup kitchen, afterschool activities for teens, and counseling for its neighbors.

Staffed with only two full-time employees and a handful of volunteers, taking time off on such quick notice was out of the question. Besides, Donna reminded him so much of Kristy—

Jonas shook his head, and leaned forward again to finish tackling his email. Two quick raps, and Lana popped her head around his office door. "Kyle's here." Energetic, efficient, bobbed blonde hair bouncing, his coworker smiled, pushed up her glasses, and disappeared again. While Jonas was charged with the spiritual health of the locals, Lana took care of the day-to-day running of the operation.

Jonas shoved his chair back from the desk and got up. Much better than sorting through email. This is what Jonas loved; working with people—not the blue-glow screen of his demanding inbox. He dragged his chair around to the front of the desk so he could sit next to Kyle.

Following a tentative knock, the door opened. "Come on in, Kyle!" Jonas grinned and motioned the teen toward the chair.

Slim and stoop shouldered—the hallmark of a recent growth spurt—Kyle glanced at Jonas through his bangs. "Thanks, man," he said, and looked away. He chewed on his bottom lip while fiddling with the strap of his backpack.

Jonas waited while it seemed Kyle was considering something. Maybe second-guessing setting up this little chat. But then he slid the backpack off his shoulder where it hit the floor and flopped into the chair.

"You good?"

Kyle nodded, shifted a bit. His long fingers began rhythmically tapping his knee.

"What's going on? You said you wanted to talk about your dad..." Jonas leaned back in his chair, unrushed but attentive.

"Yeah." Kyle sighed. "I don't know what to do, man." He clasped his hands together, like he was trying to stop the nervous tapping. But his leg picked up the rhythm, knee bouncing. "He wants to see me..."

"Okay...and?"

Kyle glared at Jonas. "I'm still mad at him. He left me. Us. It really hurt Mom. No word—just not there one day. Poof. Gone."

Kyle's story was not unusual. Absentee fathers were all too common in the community. Jonas glanced at his family picture on the desk. It wasn't right. Men just walking away. The kids deserved better.

"You're angry that he left you."

Kyle rushed on. "Yeah, man. Why'd he do that? And now...now he just wants me to pretend it never happened?"

"Is that what he said?"

"No. He asked me to forgive him or some shit." Kyle jutted his chin out.

"Do you think he is genuinely sorry?"

"Sure, but what difference does that make? Doesn't change what he did." He swallowed hard.

"No, you're right." Jonas nodded, thoughtful for a moment. "There is nothing he can do to change the past." He paused. "I think that's where forgiveness comes in. It's like saying 'I can't change what I did, but I *am* sorry. Do over?'"

"I dunno."

"The other side of forgiveness is for you."

"Me?"

"Yep. Even when a person that hurt you isn't sorry, you can forgive them."

Kyle snorted. "Why would I do that?"

"Because the anger festers in here." He clutched his shirt by his heart. "It morphs into something ugly and eats you alive." A feeling of recognition flared in his mind. The detective saying "cold case." Hollow promises not to forget it. No—not going there. Jonas shoved it away and focused back on Kyle.

"Yeah, maybe." Kyle deflated.

"How about this? Take your time and think about it, but instead of telling your dad 'no,' just say 'not yet.'"

Kyle, staring out the window, scratched at his neck. He dropped his hand and looked back at Jonas. "Yeah, I could do that."

Jonas wrapped up their talk and sent Kyle out to the dining room to get some breakfast before school. He moved his chair back to the desk and sat down. The laptop screen had gone dark.

His reflection in the glass frowned.

"Enough...," he muttered and clicked the mouse to wake up the screen. The face disappeared.

Jonas scrolled down through his remaining emails to the last one. It was from Michael, the Regional Director of Grace Ministries. His boss.

He opened it.

Good morning, Jonas!

I have an exciting opportunity to share with you. We've been struggling to find a suitable candidate to place at Dagonport State Correctional Facility as chaplain. We have a need there currently that is time-critical.

Because you have a background in pastoral care, and Grace Street is humming along just fine, I am redirecting you to Dagonport for a week or two. Lana can hold down the fort for you in your absence. We'll send her some extra volunteers.

The specific need is for the death row inmates. There are thirteen men incarcerated in that cell block currently, but one in particular—Isaiah Jackson—is scheduled for execution in November. His final appeal has been denied. I want you to minister to him specifically but also to all the men in general, as needed.

Plan to arrive on Monday. I'll have all the paperwork

taken care of prior to your arrival. May God bless you, and don't hesitate to reach out if you have questions.

Grace and Peace,
Michael

Jonas leaned back in his chair still gripping the mouse. "You have got to be kidding me..." He dragged a hand through his hair. Give pastoral care to death row criminals? There was no way...

Jonas leaned forward, closed out his inbox, and opened a browser. He typed "Isaiah Jackson" into the search bar. He'd never heard of him, but he'd find out what this guy was being executed for.

A photo popped up on the search page. Isaiah Jackson. A mugshot from fifteen years earlier. Young guy, snarling dragon tattoos clawing their way up his neck. Stone cold eyes. Oh, yeah. This guy was a winner.

Jonas clicked on the first article listed.

He skimmed over the appeals history. Don't care. What did you do, Isaiah?

"Isaiah Jackson was convicted almost fifteen years ago... double homicide of Sandra Lehigh, 30, and her son Spencer, 6..."

Cold tendrils slithered down his spine. Oh, God. Kristy had been thirty. Tyler, seven. Too close.

Morning light flashed off the picture frame. He squinted. Shifted so the computer screen blocked it.

He should close the browser. He kept reading.

“...searching for drug money...the crime scene showed excessive brutality...shot and stabbed...”

His mind blanked, awash in blue ice.

He inhaled, but his lungs wouldn't expand. Tight and shrinking. He leaned forward, placing both hands on the desk. Shallow breaths panted past his lips. They felt numb. Cold. His vision began to narrow, the edges going dark.

He closed his eyes. *Breathe slowly. In. Out. Slowly.* His lungs began to expand a little. In. Out. Inch by inch, he pushed back the vice gripping him.

After a few minutes, he felt grounded in his chair again, his breathing normalizing. He opened his eyes and leaned back. The computer screen began to come into focus.

He eased the laptop closed, his hand staying on top as if to keep Isaiah Jackson locked inside.

CHAPTER TWO

JONAS WENT THROUGH HIS DAY, a buzzing in the back of his head and the tips of his fingers numb. He'd been unable to concentrate while playing chess with one of the retirees. He'd moved the pieces without thinking and lost his king in record time. The man had lifted an eyebrow but was happy enough to claim the victory. He tried relocating to the kitchen. After the third time he'd fumbled a dish while prepping for the lunch crowd, Lana spoke up.

"You okay? You seem out of sorts."

He carefully set the pan he was holding onto the counter. "I'm fine."

Lana leaned her hip against the counter, crossed her arms, and did the "I'm waiting" thing with her eyes.

The deep fryer sizzled. The aroma of french fries filled the kitchen.

Jonas sighed. "My head's just in a bit of a fog. It'll pass."

"Oh, no. You've probably got germs ready to blow into a summer cold. You'll infect us all." She reached over and slid the pan away from him. "Shoo! Go home. The girls and I will take care of this."

"You're being bossy, Miss Lana."

Lana arched a single eyebrow. Her range of facial expressions was unparalleled. The corner of her mouth tipped up. "I'm serious. You work too hard. Just take the afternoon, relax. It's Friday, so get a head start on your weekend." Picking up the pan, she looked over her shoulder at him. "I'll exact my pound of flesh from you on Monday." She winked and was gone.

Jonas chuckled but then felt the oppressive weight from earlier land back on his mind. A suffocating blanket of anger and sadness woven together. He scrubbed both hands through his hair. "Yeah. Yeah, I'm going," he said to the empty kitchen.

On the drive home, Jonas's thoughts bounced chaotically between memories of his wife and son, the frustration of their killer or killers having never been caught, and, frankly, the gall of Michael to redirect him to minister to the rabid animals at Dagonport death row. Rabid animals get put down. That's mercy.

Taillights flashed red in front of him approaching a stoplight. Jonas slowed, realizing he'd been on autopilot while driving, his mind twisting this way and that, buffeted by the sudden onslaught of emotions. His hands had been clenching and releasing the steering wheel, over and over. Stretching his fingers to relax them, he focused on his driving.

Just as the light turned green, it occurred to him he'd forgotten to mention the email from Michael to Lana—she was expecting him back Monday. And he'd never responded to

Michael's email; not that it had been a request awaiting an answer.

Once home, Jonas headed to the living room. Nested chairs and a couch meant for a family sat empty. The TV dark. Games stacked on a bookshelf, untouched. Lifeless.

Jonas sat on the couch, yanking at the knot of his tie as he laid his head back. Family photos hung on the wall watching him, memories trapped in a moment.

He stared at the ceiling, willing his mind to stop racing, to become blank again. So much easier than processing the chaos that clawed at the inside of his skull.

After a few deep breaths, he heard laughter. Lifting his head, he looked toward the dining room. He saw himself, Kristy, and Tyler sitting around the table.

"What do you call a blind buck?" Tyler bounced in his seat, practicing not blowing the punchline by shouting it out right away.

Grinning, Jonas very slowly reached for the bowl of mashed potatoes. Getting the timing just right on joke delivery was important business.

"Come on, Dad! Say your part!"

Jonas scooped out some potatoes onto his plate and set down the bowl. "I don't know, Tyler. What do you call a blind buck?"

"No-eyed deer!" Tyler jumped up. "Do you get it? No-eyed deer, no idea?" He cackled and flopped back into his chair.

Chuckling, Kristy turned to Jonas. "The delivery is much improved. Maybe move to the lesson on not explaining your joke next." She smiled at Tyler. "That was a good one. I haven't heard it before."

Jonas reached over and ruffled Tyler's hair. "That was great, buddy. How about one more, then we concentrate on dinner."

Tyler's eyes lit up. "Yes, yes, yes!" He looked toward the ceiling for a moment. Then his head snapped back down. "I got one... What did one eye say to the other eye?"

Kristy poured ice water from a pitcher into their glasses. "I'm detecting an 'eye' theme tonight."

"What did *one eye say to the other eye?" Jonas asked.*

"Between you and me, something smells!" Tyler burst out laughing. "Do you get it? Smells, a nose—"

Tyler's laughter moved further away. Turned sharp.

The vision blinked out. A clock ticked.

Jonas leaned forward as sobs tore out from deep within. He plucked at his shirt, over and over—trying to release the stranglehold on his chest.

Outside, the sun set.

CHAPTER THREE

SUNDAY MORNING JONAS stood at the kitchen sink looking out the window, coffee mug in hand, forgotten. Raindrops hit the window. They joined together forming rivulets that meandered down the glass, merging with other rivulets—becoming more confident and determined—picking up speed and streaming off the bottom pane, out of sight.

Setting the mug in the sink after swallowing the last of the coffee, he leaned forward. He tried to focus past the rain-streaked window, through to the outside. Just gray-green smudge. Nothing clear. He didn't try very hard.

He turned around, leaned back against the sink, arms crossed over his chest. He had a decision to make. At some level, he suspected he'd already made it.

The day before he'd found himself sitting cross-legged on the bedroom floor. The closet door yawned open, the box he'd dragged out sat in front of him.

Jonas looked into the box of neatly organized documents. Somehow color-coded files and indexing would bring the killer to justice sooner.

He reached in and pulled out the top folder—news clippings. The first headline shouted, "Family Slain...Killer(s) Unknown." He ran his fingers over the grainy black and white photo of Kristy and Tyler posing together beneath it. Kristy would be mortified to know that her ugly Christmas sweater —a family tradition—had made it into the newspaper. He inhaled deeply through his nose and closed the folder.

He picked up the next one. Police reports and crime scene photos. He'd been given the ones after their bodies had been removed. He examined one for the hundredth time. Full color and sharp. Thick blood pooled on the floor. Soaked into the carpet. He leaned back and looked at the ceiling.

He pushed that folder away.

Grabbed the next one. Autopsy. A diagram of a generic female body. Arrows like bullets to her head. Precise angle, exact range. He slammed it shut.

His gut cramping, Jonas shoved the papers back in the box. Tyler and Kristy's murder reduced to paperwork, his fortress built from it. He kicked the box away.

Silence stilled the air.

He stood, walked out, and closed the bedroom door behind him.

Jonas pushed off from the sink and headed to the dining room. Last night before going to bed, he'd sent Michael a response.

Michael,

I appreciate your confidence in me. Due to the trauma I still face daily from the murder of my wife and child, I am not the right fit for this prison ministry assignment.

Sincerely,
Jonas

He walked into the dining room and stopped. The room was silent, the table bare of anything except his closed laptop. He clenched his fists and looked at the ceiling, squeezing his eyes shut to stop the building pressure of tears. Shaking it off, he looked back at the laptop. Michael was reasonable, a good boss, a man of God.

He pulled out the chair, sat down, and booted up the computer. He tapped his fingers on the table as he waited for the inbox to show up, the mechanics whirring as it loaded. There, it was up. Jonas watched as the messages were retrieved, his eyes instantly landing on one from Michael. He tapped on the message.

Jonas,

I understand your reluctance. But it is precisely because of the loss of Kristy and Tyler that I believe the Lord is calling you to His work at Dagonport. You are in a position to meaningfully offer these men the truth of forgiveness and repentance. From another, it could just sound like lip service.

I also believe the Lord has in mind to use this as healing for you; a chance to see men who have made poor choices as fellow humans.

Remember the Lord's words: So will My word be which goes out of My mouth; It will not return to Me empty, Without accomplishing what I desire, And without succeeding in the purpose for which I sent it.

The assignment stands. They will be expecting you at Dagonport tomorrow.

Sincerely,
Michael

Jonas slammed the lid down and shoved the laptop crashing to the ground. How could Michael...No, how could *God* do this to him?

The laptop fan whirred and then fell silent.

He stormed through the house, an enraged bull. A picture frame rattled against the wall. Enraged at God. After Kristy and Tyler's death he had *dedicated* his life to Grace Street. Ministering to hundreds of lost or worn-down souls. Day in, day out. For years.

Why wasn't that *enough*?

But to send him to death row? To offer salvation to the killers...

Jonas laughed as he fell back into a living room chair. The

laugh transformed into a hoarse bellow. He scrubbed his face with his hands. That's just not happening.

The room shrank. He needed to get out.

A leave of absence. He would just...*go*. What could they do? Fire him? It just didn't matter anymore.

He forced himself to slow down, to sift through the static. He searched for a lifeline. A thread. An excuse.

"Donna!" Jonas jumped up and headed to the dining room. "I'm coming, Phil. I'll be there for your graduation." He scooped the laptop off the floor and sat down at the table.

The screen had a starburst crack in the center. *No, no, no.* Jonas jabbed at the power button and sat back when it whirred to life. But the screen didn't light up. He stared at his reflection through fragmented flashing pixels. *Come on.* The activity settled, and Jonas was left staring at a dark screen with a single white line across the middle. He waited.

He slammed the lid closed. He retrieved his phone and went upstairs. He needed to call Grace Street and leave a message for Lana. No one would answer today because it was Sunday. Good.

He began yanking clothes out of his closet as the voicemail greeting finished. "Lana, it's Jonas." His voice quaked. "There has been a family emergency. I need to leave town. I don't know when I'll be back. Please tell Michael that I'm filing for a leave of absence, unspecified length of time." Pressing the off button, he tossed the phone on the bed.

He grabbed a duffel bag and started shoving clothes in. Pants. He'd dedicated his life to these people. Shirts. To God. Underwear. How could they ask him to do this? Socks. His wife and kid were dead. Toothbrush. This was outrageous. He yanked the zipper closed.

Jonas grabbed his duffel and phone. He pounded down the stairs, snatched a jacket off the coat rack, scooped up his car keys, and walked out.

Lawnview Cemetery was a palette of green layered over green swathes—saturated and dripping from the persistent drizzle.

Jonas stood very still, his hand resting on the cold, wet granite headstone. Water seeping from his hair, under his collar, trickled down his back. His thoughts were white static.

He crouched down in front of the stone and trailed his fingers over Kristy's name. He waited for powerful emotion to surge forward, but there was…nothing. Water trickled over his hand.

Jonas stood up and walked over to Tyler's smaller stone. Rain dripped from his nose. "I miss you, buddy." He stepped back, turned, and headed to his car.

Sitting in his car, parked to the side of the cemetery lane, Jonas leaned his head against the side window. He searched through the static to try and find the threads for a coherent thought.

Donna. He needed to call her.

He picked up his cell and placed the call.

"Hello? Jonas, is that you?"

"Hey, Donna. I, um, just wanted to let you know I got your email, and I would love to come to Phil's graduation."

"Is everything okay? You sound funny."

"I'm fine. Just tired. Work's been tough."

"Well, I'm thrilled you're coming. When can we expect you?"

Jonas looked at the windshield, the rain heavier now, drumming on the car roof, blurring his view.

"I'm leaving now."

"Tonight?"

"Yeah. I mean, I'll stop and get a motel room along the way, so I'd get to you tomorrow."

Donna didn't answer right away. "Jonas, what's really going on?"

Through the watery blur of the windshield, he could see the stiff gray lumps of headstones lined up perfectly in rows.

He swallowed. "I'm at the cemetery," he said quietly. "I just... I just need to get away for a bit."

"That's fine. Please come here. But Jonas, I don't want you driving. You sound wrung out and it's late. Why don't you take the bus, get some rest on the way?"

Donna was right. His body felt heavy and numb, depleted. He would be able to just shut down for a few hours.

Jonas agreed to text her the arrival time. He started the car and headed downtown to the bus station.

CHAPTER FOUR

EARL PARKER ZIPPED up his suitcase, popped out the extendable handle, and pulled it off the bed. He rolled it behind him out the bedroom door and down the hall. Setting it by the front door, he called up the weather app on his phone. *Rain, heavy at times. 78 degrees.* Ugh. Wet and muggy. He sifted through his coats, nabbing the blue jacket that would keep him mostly dry and not make him sweat through his shirt in under five minutes. He laid the jacket on top of the suitcase and headed to say goodbye to his family.

He stuck his head through the family room door. The room was dark except for the glow of the TV; they were watching Titanic for the umpteenth time. Victor Garber was reassuring Kate Winslet on screen. Earl flipped on the light and walked into the room, voice booming in perfect sync, "Sleep soundly, young Rose. I have built you a good ship, strong and true—"

"Da-aad! Why do you always do that?" Siobhan, his

daughter in the throes of the teenage drama stage, shrieked at him.

Earl's wife, Lindy, laughed and paused the movie.

Earl turned to Siobhan. "Because it is a fantastic line, and later, when it sinks—"

"DAD! You just gave away the ending!" She threw herself back on the couch with a flourish of arms.

Earl looked at his wife. "Did she not remember the movie's ending from the twenty other times she's seen it? Did she not learn about this event in school?"

Lindy stood up and reached for Earl, wrapping her arms around his neck. "It's like a ritual. We pretend we don't remember, so it's all new and exciting each time." She leaned forward and kissed him. "You taking off now?"

"I am. I'll be back in a week." He hugged Lindy.

He turned to Siobhan, who was now covering her eyes at the gross spectacle of parental PDA. "Come here, sweetheart. Give me a hug."

She bounced off the couch into Earl's open arms, squeezing him tight. "Why do you have to go for so long?" she mumbled into his shirt.

"It's required training. Maybe there will be a raise at some point when I show off my shiny, new skills." He kissed her forehead. "I'll be back well in time for your birthday."

"In time to buy me a present for my birthday?"

Earl snorted. He grabbed both of his girls into one last bear hug, then headed out into the rainy evening.

After parking in the passenger lot, Earl walked to the macadam area where the bus was loading. Harsh sodium lamps lit the space—white spotlights shining down from a blackening sky—making it feel later than it actually was. He pulled his ball cap further down his forehead to block the steady rain, his suitcase trundling along behind him.

After passing his case to the worker loading luggage into the belly of the bus, Earl pulled out his phone and showed his e-ticket to the driver. "A good misty, moisty evening to you, sir!"

The driver chuckled as he scanned the ticket. "That it is. Climb on up; we depart in a few minutes."

Earl mounted the three steps up, removed his cap, then surveyed the passengers on board in search of a likely traveling companion to talk to; he hated sitting alone. The people were scattered about, the bus only a third full. Everyone looked fairly dull—solo travelers who had put a purse or bag on the empty seat beside them, probably to discourage any interaction.

Earl saw a young boy, bouncing in his seat with puppy-like enthusiasm, about half way back, tossing a white ball from hand to hand. A first time bus trip perhaps. How exciting for him! He'd be fun to talk to, but a woman, presumably his mom, sat next to him by the window, busily tapping on her phone.

Behind the boy, across the aisle, a man leaned against the window, staring into the rainy night. He looked so sad. No... *lost*. Earl checked the seat next to the man. No bag or book. Practically an invitation.

Earl's plan fixed in his mind—sit by the sad man to cheer him, and he'd still be catty-corner from the bouncy boy—he turned slightly sideways to navigate the aisle. Were the aisles always this narrow? Maybe he had grown wider. He chuckled at himself. Anyone who glanced his way was treated to a "good evening!"

When Earl reached the boy's seat, he grinned. "Hello there, young man!"

The boy smiled right back. "Hi! I'm Jamie." Bounce, bounce, bounce.

"It's a pleasure to meet you, Jamie. My name is Earl." They shook hands. "Is this your first time on a bus?"

"No, of course not." Jamie's laugh was delightful. "I'm in Kindergarten. I take the bus every day. Well, not Saturday and Sunday. And not on holidays. But all the other days." He leaned forward and whispered, "but it's my first time on a bus with a potty." He motioned his head toward the back.

"Indeed!" Earl noticed the woman looking at him. He reached out his hand. "Jamie's mother, I presume."

She nodded and shook his hand. "I'm sorry, he can be a real chatterbox at times."

"Not at all," Earl shook his head. "Jamie, you can talk to me as much as you'd like. I think I'll be sitting near you."

Jamie beamed.

Earl patted him on the shoulder, and took a step farther on. He looked at the sad man staring out the window. Everything about this man was the opposite of Jamie.

"Excuse me. Would you mind if I sit here?"

The man didn't move at first, then seemed to pull himself

from whatever far away place he'd gone. "What? Oh, yeah. Sure."

Earl stuck out his hand, "I'm Earl."

The man shook it. "Jonas." His face was still blank.

Earl settled into his seat, confident that he'd chosen well.

The bus driver turned off the overhead lights, put the bus in gear, and off they went.

After fifteen or twenty minutes, the bus pulled onto the turnpike, settling into a monotonous rhythm. The road thrummed beneath them, oversized wiper blades swished like a metronome, rain beat against the windows in a steady cadence.

Outside was pitch black, only a blurry pair of red lights appearing occasionally as the bus passed a car. Inside was dark, with bright islands where passengers had turned on the overhead reading light.

Earl looked at these spotlighted areas to study the people, but it was difficult between the high seat backs and seeing only the back of their heads. Next to him, Jonas sat up and shifted in his seat. Earl seized the opening.

"So Jonas." Earl turned toward him a bit. "Where are you headed?"

Jonas scrubbed at his cheek. "Cincinnati. You?"

Earl, delighted that Jonas was engaging now, smiled. "Farther along. Chicago. I have a conference there for work. Kind of a drag to travel so far, but I'm excited about some of the workshops. We have some meet-and-greets to share ideas. It should be good." Earl couldn't tell if Jonas was actually listening. "What's in Cincy?"

Jonas cleared his throat. "My sister-in-law and her family. My nephew Phil is graduating high school, so I'm going to visit for that."

"Ah, a teenager. That's really great. Good for him. Hey, maybe you can help me brainstorm an idea. My daughter Siobhan is 13. I love her to pieces, but man oh man, with that puberty and all, it's like tiptoeing on eggshells through a minefield." Earl laughed. "Oops, I think I mixed my metaphor there." He glanced at Jonas. He was losing him. "Anyway, she's turning 14 next week. She won't tell me what she wants for a gift, because *somehow* I already should know. Do you have any suggestions for what to get a blossoming young lady, who knows way more than her parents, for her birthday?"

Jonas stared at Earl. He looked confused. Or trapped. Earl berated himself. Why did he talk so much? Jonas looked like he'd been steamrolled.

Earl chuckled and tugged at his collar. "It's okay. I'll figure it out in Chicago." He swallowed. "You have kids, Jonas?"

Jonas slowly turned his gaze forward and leaned his head against the window. Earl could barely hear him. "I had a wife and son. They're dead."

The breath whooshed out of Earl.

"Jonas. I am so very sorry." Dear God, that explained why this man was lost. He had been devastated. Earl knew he should shut up, leave this poor guy alone. But he couldn't stop himself. "Was it an accident? Like a car accident?"

Jonas lifted his head from the glass and turned toward Earl. He looked more present than he had so far. “No. My wife and my boy were murdered, slaughtered in our home. The dog, too.” He swallowed hard. “The killer got away. He gets to live, free and clear. And now,” Jonas looked up and raised his hand slightly, “God thinks…me. That I should be the one.” He paused. “That I should be the one to share mercy with them.”

Jonas shook his head. He lowered his hand and looked back at Earl. Tears glittered in his eyes. Earl had no idea what to say. Jonas continued, “If it’s okay, I think I'd like to get some sleep.”

Earl nodded, and Jonas leaned over against the window and closed his eyes. Earl, still nodding, looked down at his hands. Clasped them together. Pulled them apart. He leaned back in his chair, exhaling quietly.

CHAPTER FIVE

SOME TIME LATER, Jonas woke up. He searched for what had awakened him. The bus sailed smoothly over the road, rain rhythmically pounding down. The interior was quiet, only a few overhead lights shone. His bladder. He needed to go.

He turned toward the man seated next to him. What was his name? He looked like he was resting but not asleep. Earl. "Excuse me," croaked from his dry throat. He cleared it, and Earl looked over offering a tentative smile. "Earl, I need to use the bathroom. Sorry to bother you..."

"Oh, oh, of course!" Earl got up, joints popping and cracking. He stepped forward till he was even with seats ahead of them. Jonas slipped by and headed to the lavatory at the rear of the bus.

Jonas came out of the bathroom. The passengers slept in the dark, except in one spotlight ahead. Earl leaned against a seat talking to a young boy. Jonas walked down the aisle, hand over hand on the seat backs, eyes drawn to the warm tableau of Earl listening intently to the boy's chatter.

As Jonas got closer, he could see more of the boy. Laughing, tossing a white ball from hand to hand, arcing back and forth…

Tyler in the backyard, laughing as he tossed a white ball. Kiki streaking across to catch it. Returning to Tyler triumphant, her black ears flapping with each stride, white heart on her forehead bobbing and tail wagging.

Jonas smiled. He rubbed at the fierce warmth in his chest.

The dark bus came rushing back in. Earl talking to the boy in the spotlight. Jonas dropped his hand, the image of Tyler and Kiki rushing away from him. He stood there a moment, empty.

"Everything good, Jonas?" Earl smiled at him.

He nodded and took the last few steps to his seat and sat before his legs gave out. He felt Earl get comfortable next to him, but he kept his gaze aimed toward the stormy darkness.

After a few moments, he could hear something low and melodic. He strained to hear it, to separate it from the thrumming rain. Earl was singing softly. Jonas closed his eyes as the honey tones washed over him. His fists unclenched as he sagged deeper into the seat, then nothing.

CHAPTER SIX

JONAS STRUGGLED UPWARD out of his dark place. Stripes of yellow-orange flashed across his eyelids. Groggily, he opened his eyes. They were traveling through one of the tunnels that had been blasted through the mountains. Sodium vapor lamps emitting an intense yellow lined the tunnel. The pounding rain and road noise had been replaced with a harsh hollow vibration. Jonas realized he was counting the light bars as they streaked by, the remaining rivulets of rain on the window absorbing and distorting the color.

After a full minute, the light abruptly stopped, plunging the bus back into the dark rainy night. In the bus's headlights, Jonas could make out the road ahead as it veered sharply to the left after exiting the tunnel, following the curve of the mountainside.

In a moment, time stretched. The road noise silenced.

They were hydroplaning—the bus gliding, eerily smooth, like skating on glass. Jonas stared at the curve ahead with acid crawling up his throat. They weren't going to make it. The bus was going full speed and beginning to fishtail.

Then nothing beneath them. Weightless. Silent.

The bus slammed onto the embankment and Jonas's teeth cracked together. He grabbed the seat in front of him as the bus jerked and bucked down the slope into darkness. Sleeping passengers were thrown forward.

Jonas looked over at Earl who was also gripping the seat back. He was peering around the seat down the aisle. "What do you see?" Jonas forced out between clenched teeth.

"It looks like a field with some trees, maybe an orchard." Earl glanced at him. "I think we are slowing down."

Well, not fast enough.

"Wait," his voice quivered. "There's something black up ahead—"

The bus leapt another embankment and slammed into water. Jonas crashed into the seat ahead, shoulder and chest taking the blow. A wall of black swallowed the windshield.

The screaming stopped.

CHAPTER SEVEN

TWIN LIGHTS SHONE into thick darkness, bits of detritus floating through the yellow beams. The wipers dragged across the windshield in slow, groaning arcs, the motor whining from the strain. Rain thrummed against the roof—but not the windshield. Flicking his gaze upward, the driver saw a water-line, lapping at the window. The bus bobbed and swayed beneath him.

The front of the bus was partially submerged.

The driver, Hank Anderson, shut off the engine and turned on the interior lights. Water streamed into the stairwell by the door—already several inches deep. Groans and soft weeping reached him as he struggled with his seatbelt. "Folks, is every-body okay?" The bus had pitched forward, the angle making it difficult for him to stand without falling against the steering wheel.

Turning and standing while holding onto the first pair of seatbacks, Hank scanned the passengers. "Is anybody injured?" They looked terrified and shaken but not hurt.

"We're in the water. Are we going to drown?" A woman a few seats back looked at him with wide eyes.

Hank raised a hand. "No. Nobody is going to drown. It feels like the rear wheels are still on dry ground in the back. Just the front is in the water." He tore his gaze from the woman and made eye contact with the rest of passengers—one by one—as he continued speaking. "The front door is no longer accessible. I'm going to open the emergency hatch in the roof. I'm going to get each and every one of you out onto dry land."

A man halfway back stood up. "How can I help? I want to help. Name's Earl."

Hank smiled. "Yes, sir. Earl, I accept your help."

The bus jerked forward, knocking Hank up the aisle a few steps. It slid slowly, tipping at a greater angle. The lights flickered. Hank turned and lurched back to his seat and grabbed a flashlight. The overhead lights winked out. The sensation—the belly of the bus grinding over the edge, then becoming buoyant in total darkness—triggered wailing from the passengers.

Turning on the flashlight, Hank took several deep breaths. "Stay calm, everybody." His heart pounded. The bus jolted again, stopping suddenly. Still anchored in the back.

Hank pulled himself along the aisle by the seat backs. "Everybody stay seated. We'll be getting off in a jiffy. If you have a light on your phone, turn it on." He reached the middle of the bus. "Earl, I need you to help hold me while I unlatch this." He pointed the flashlight toward the hatch.

Hank awkwardly clambered onto two seats straddling the

aisle, while Earl supported his legs. He kept speaking as he worked the mechanism. "I'm going to climb on top, take a quick look around to identify the best place to offload. Then you help people get up to me. Send an adult first who can help from the bank. Good?" He pushed open the hatch on squealing hinges till it banged against the top of the bus.

"Sounds good."

Hank passed Earl his flashlight and hoisted himself up. Lying flat on the roof, he reached back in for his flashlight. He stood, balancing carefully on the slanted roof, and swung the light in an arc to get an idea of what had happened and how he was going to rescue twenty-some people before the bus slid in completely.

The water looked to be a lake of some sort—maybe a reservoir—but it was difficult to tell in the narrow shaft of light. The rear axle of the bus had snagged on a crumbling retaining wall. The broken chunks of concrete did not look substantial.

Hank lay back down to talk to Earl. A young man stepped forward, nodding at Earl. "Okay, offloading will be fairly easy. The bank rises in such a way to make it a short jump." He looked at the young man. "Are you up for helping others make that jump?"

"Absolutely."

"Then let's go."

Earl helped the man climb up till he could hoist himself out.

Hank stuck his head back in through the opening and said

quietly, "Earl, we need to keep this moving quickly. Orderly, but fast."

Earl nodded.

Hank showed the first man where to jump to shore, waited for him to turn on his phone light, and returned to the hatch.

"Who have we here?" Hank smiled at the young boy.

"I'm Jamie. Earl said I could go next."

"Earl was right. Up you go." Earl lifted and Hank grabbed him. He showed Jamie where to jump.

Next came the boy's mother. The water had made its way up the aisle and was lapping at her ankles. Then one after another, Earl kept them coming through the hatch, whether they could lift themselves out or needed to be lifted and handed to Hank.

"How many left?"

Earl looked around the bus, bright cellphone lights blinding him. "Maybe five? The water is up to our knees."

"OK. I can see red and blue lights up the hill on the highway. Help should be here momentarily."

The bus jerked. Hank swung the flashlight down—the retaining wall was crumbling, chunks splashing into the black water. The bus was going in.

"Get everyone to the back of the bus. Then lift them up as fast as you can, Earl. Let's go!"

Hank heard Earl urging everyone to move. Then Earl and Hank got the next person up. Then two more. All safe on land. Just two left inside. With a swoop, the bus slipped free, all friction vanishing. Hank lost his grip and slid across the slick surface, splashing into the frigid water.

Earl, standing on a seat at an awkward angle, lost his balance and fell into the aisle. The frame of the bus groaned under increasing water pressure. Metal screeched and glass shattered. Earl scrambled to his feet, sloshing in the rising water, and looked toward the sound. It was pitch black, but the sound had come from the front. The door had caved in. The bus would fill rapidly now, and it was going down head first.

Looking out the window, through murky water, Earl saw Hank's flashlight bob, then rise—he'd made it to shore.

Earl waded, pulling himself up the aisle, to the last passenger. He could just make out the outline of Jonas from the gray light leaking through the hatch. Jonas still sat in his seat, arms braced against the seat in front of him. Staring at it. Oblivious to the water lapping at his waist. "Jonas! Get up—we need to get out now!"

Jonas turned his head slowly toward Earl. "This is all my fault," he mumbled.

"Jonas!"

Jonas struggled to stand and nodded at Earl. Earl grabbed his arm. "I'll hoist you up. Grab the edge, and I'll push."

"No." Jonas yanked his arm back. "You won't be able to get yourself up then. I'll lift you."

"I'm not leaving you here, buddy!" Water began to pour in one side of the hatch as the bus submerged.

"I can swim. You go."

Jonas shoved him toward the seat beneath the hatch.

"You have a birthday party to get to."

Earl hesitated.

"Go."

Earl clambered up and gripped the edge of the hatch as water poured down over him. Jonas's hands were at his back for a moment—then gone. Earl pulled himself up and out. In the rush of water, Earl was swept off. He waited, treading water, scanning for a shape, a splash, anything. Nothing broke the surface. The reservoir swallowed the bus.

ACT II

CHAPTER EIGHT

WHITE STRETCHED.

Featureless. Endless. Anchored. Solid. Bluish white. The man walked, his steps echoing. But how were they echoing? He searched for a wall, for a shadow, but there were none. He looked up to the ceiling, but whiteness soared as far as he could see. He kept walking but got no closer to anything. He turned around, walking backward, but he got no farther from anything. The man simply existed in the center of the White, in the center of everything, in the center of nothing.

He kept walking, even with no destination within his grasp. How else would time be marked and space measured? What if he stopped moving, and time and space collapsed, folded in and smothered him? His footsteps—their echoes—kept him grounded.

Who was he? Step, step, step, step. He searched his mind though it was as void as his space.

Step, step, Jonas, Jonas. He was Jonas. That *felt* right. Jonas, Jonas, Jonas, Jonas.

"Jonas! Can you hear me?" The paramedic stared at the flat white line on his monitor. The whir of a machine winding up cut through the night. "Hit him again." Paddles delivered a current of electricity to Jonas's heart. Blue and red strobe lights from a dozen emergency vehicles revolved, the beams chopped up by tree trunks that stood against them. Jonas's body arched from the ground in a tremendous spasm, then flopped back down on the muddy shore.

Bus passengers stood huddled in knots, wrapped in blankets, watching the battle for a man's life. Prayers could be heard, murmurs to God. They pleaded for mercy for this stranger and offered thanks that they'd been spared. The rain had abated—only a drizzle now—speckling faces and dripping from eyelashes.

"We've got a rhythm. Let's move him out of here!" Paramedics lifted Jonas onto a gurney, extended its collapsed legs, and began the bumpy trip back up the incline the bus had traveled down. "We've got you, Jonas."

Jonas, Jonas, Jonas, Jonas. Measured steps across a vast, sterile tundra. A memory alighted—flapping, unsure—then settled itself. One, and then another, jostling for space. He examined them, one at a time, tasting each to see if it was familiar. They gathered—a piece, a thread, with each step—becoming a coherent tapestry of his past. They gave him a touchstone to orient himself within this other-worldly landscape. They created boundaries for his mind so that it wouldn't cast itself into the White.

The ICU hummed with its own late-night rhythm. Sterile and calm, it promised to keep the demons at bay. A centrally located nurse's station—a lit island in an otherwise shadowy ward—acted as the nerve center, receiving and processing electronic input from the rooms that surrounded it.

Donna sat stiff-backed in a chair by Jonas's bed. An overbed light illuminated his marble-pale face. A ventilator huffing —a push and pull of air—breathed for him, while monitors beeped and dinged and chirped sending volumes of information to the nurse's station. Donna's gaze bounced between his lifeless face and the bewildering array of digital output on a monitor at the head of the bed. None of those machines would be making noise if Jonas were dead.

Over time, after a hundred steps or a thousand steps—Jonas didn't know—the tone of the echoes began to shift. They sounded increasingly like a human voice. Jonas halted. It was the first time he'd stopped walking since arriving in the White. The echoes stopped. He sensed he wasn't alone, but turning in a full circle revealed nothing.

"Jonas."

Jonas looked around again; he looked up. Where was that coming from? Was it even coming from out there or was it inside his mind? He couldn't tell. “Who are you? Where am I?”

“Sit down, Jonas. I will hold the space for you.”

“Michael?” Jonas sat and was surprised to find a wall behind him to lean against. “You sound like Michael.”

"Michael speaks for me.”

And then nothing.

Jonas rocked back and forth, rubbing his forehead as the silence stretched, blending with the vast whiteness. "You were never going to let me run away, were you?”

"I love you too much to do that.”

"If you love me, why did you take my wife and child?” Searing pinpricks peppered the collage of memories behind his eyes, glowing with life for a moment before flaring, then turning to smoldering ashes—felt, but no longer seen. Defenses collapsing, Jonas cried.

He cried for Tyler and Kristy. He cried for himself. He was a hot coal of agony adrift in a void.

The back of Donna’s throat burned as she struggled to hold back tears. Jonas was family, but he meant more than that—he was the final tether to her sister. She and Kristy had been close, sharing the unpredictability of their teen years, and later, the failures and successes of married life and raising kids. Late night conversations in their shared bedroom—decorated with posters of travel fantasies from the crystal turquoise Aegean waters to the humming nightlife of a European city—morphed into long talks on the phone as they'd left home and moved several states apart.

That had been ripped away with Kristy and Tyler's murder. Donna and Jonas still held and protected the shredded pieces of those lives. Without Jonas, Donna feared the scraps would blow away never to be held again.

She leaned forward with her face pushed against the blanket on the hospital bed, and cried.

▭

"Jonas."

The voice grounded Jonas. Wiping his wet face and inhaling deeply, he nodded.

"Do you trust me?"

"I have always—" Jonas's voice cracked. "I have followed you since I was a child. I've dedicated my life to feeding, clothing, and counseling those in need."

"In this you have trusted me. Why not the rest?"

"I don't understand why you allowed a murderer to kill my family, and then sent me to minister to murderers!"

"I've never asked you to understand. Only to trust."

CHAPTER NINE

An older man in a white coat, pushed aside the curtain that acted as a door to the rest of the ward. "Hello, I'm Dr. Wong. Are you..." he consulted his clipboard, "Donna Lightner? Jonas's next of kin?"

"Yes, I'm Donna, his sister-in-law. Can you tell me how he is?" She stood up, then sat back down again.

"Right now he is resting. He needs time to heal, and then we can evaluate him further." He glanced at his clipboard notes. "Jonas was submerged in water following the bus accident. A fellow passenger rescued him, detected no breathing or heartbeat, and performed CPR until the paramedics arrived. They restarted his heart and brought him here."

"Is he going to recover?" Donna searched for tissues in her purse but came up empty.

Grabbing a tissue box by the sink, Dr. Wong handed them to her. He dragged over another chair and sat down.

"The answer is we don't know. We don't know how long his brain was without oxygen. They estimate he was in the bus after it submerged for twenty minutes before he was rescued. We don't know if he had a pocket of air to breathe for some of that."

Donna wiped her eyes and blew her nose. "Twenty minutes is a long time without oxygen."

"In warm water, he would not have made it. But even though it is late spring, that reservoir the bus went into is fed by cold mountain water. That gives a significantly longer window of survivability."

"How long will he be unconscious?"

"He arrived in the ER unconscious. His heart rate and blood pressure were within acceptable limits. Because of water in his lungs, he struggled to breathe. He is in a medically induced coma so that the ventilator can breathe for him. We are watching for signs of brain inflammation and pneumonia. If all goes well, we can begin to pull him off the meds and the ventilator and see if he breathes easily on his own. When he wakes up we can do neurological testing." Dr. Wong paused. "Do you have any other questions?"

Jonas sat in the white space, leaning against the wall provided for him, and thought about *trust*. Did he trust God? Could he trust him?

A Bible verse memorized in childhood floated up in his mind: Trust in the Lord with all your heart, and do not lean on your own understanding. In all your ways acknowledge him, and he will make straight your paths.

He turned the words around this way and that, examining them. Four concepts: trust, Jonas's understanding was insufficient, acknowledge God, then God will make a path. He recognized the childlike trust required. Tyler didn't always understand why his parents had certain rules. And Tyler often didn't like the rules. But because of the relationship, he knew he could trust his parents to guide him.

Jonas clasped his hands together and set his chin on them. He could wrap his mind around that. He could trust God and *not* understand. He'd prefer to understand, but probably so had Tyler.

He whispered into the White, "You are my God. I will trust you with everything I have. Just as my son—whom I loved—trusted me, I trust you."

He scrubbed his face. Feeling lighter inside—the overwhelming sadness still there but quiet—he stood up. Also gone was the compulsion to hold up the space. God said he would do it and he had. God had given him a wall to lean on. Jonas realized God was caring for his needs as they arose.

CHAPTER TEN

"THE PASSENGER WHO SAVED JONAS–IS he okay?"

"Yes." He glanced back at his clipboard. "Mr. Earl Parker. He was brought to the ER also. Hypothermia. The notes report he dove back under the water several times before he was able to pull Jonas out."

Donna's throat tightened. Several times. This stranger had risked his life, over and over, refusing to give up on Jonas.

"He's warming up just fine, and his wife is on her way. I expect he'll be discharged tomorrow."

"Can I speak to him?"

"In the morning. Ask a nurse for his room number."

The following morning, Donna checked in on Jonas. There had been no change overnight. A nurse buzzed around him, changing out the IV drips and resetting switches.

Donna headed to the nurse's station. The ICU had woken up. A patient moaned on a gurney awaiting a room to be cleaned; a worker wheeled a tall metal rack with breakfast trays by her; announcements came over the loudspeaker.

"Can you give me the room number for Earl Parker?"

The nurse tapped on her keyboard. "He's in room 144, North Wing. Follow the blue line on the floor to get there."

Donna thanked her and headed toward Earl.

As Jonas stood in the White, he wondered for the first time if he were dead. This didn't match his idea of heaven—or hell, for that matter. He felt caught between layers, suspended. The conversation with God hadn't been a welcome to his eternal home, nor a condemnation for the ages. It had felt like course correction.

"Where do I go, Lord?"

In front of him, a white line appeared—the only feature in the entire void. Denser than the surrounding white, more solid, more real.

Jonas remembered: *He will make straight my paths.*

He began to follow it.

After a little while, or a long while—time still had no dimension—an object rolled across the line in front of Jonas. He paused. Up till now, nothing had moved in the White, except for him. He scanned his surroundings—white as far as he could see—then he bent over and picked up the object. A ball.

Red stitching looped the white ball. As he gripped it, it compressed slightly under his fingers—foam-soft, made for children's hands. A tee-ball. Jonas rubbed his thumb over a faint green mark. A grass stain. He gripped the ball and squeezed his eyes closed, pictures of Tyler flicking through his mind: Tyler in the backyard throwing the ball for Kiki. Jonas and Tyler tossing the ball back and forth. Kristy at Tyler's tee-ball game, scooping up a foul ball from beside her lawn chair and tossing it back to the umpire, grinning.

Donna rapped on the door to Room 144.

"Come on in and join the party!"

Donna pushed the door open and stopped. It was a full house.

"I'm Earl," a man in the hospital bed boomed with a smile. "This is my wife, Lindy, and my daughter, Siobhan—who is about to turn 14. And that young man is Jamie."

Donna stood there speechless at the overwhelming greeting. After hours of watching Jonas's lifeless body, this man was so *vibrant*.

Lindy stepped over and reached out her hand. "Don't mind Earl. He's never met a stranger." They shook hands. "Please come in and tell us who you are and what brings you here."

Donna looked from Earl's eager face, to Lindy's soft smile, to the young boy Jamie who tossed a tee-ball from one hand to another.

"I'm Donna. I'm Jonas's sister-in—" Her face crumpled, and she began sobbing. There was no holding it back.

Lindy gathered Donna into her arms and stroked her hair. "Just let it all out."

After a bit, she settled down to a few wet hiccups. "I'm so, so sorry."

Lindy led Donna to a seat and eased her into it.

Donna blew her nose and got her dignity back in order. "Thank you." Then she looked at Earl. He looked devastated.

"Did Jonas…did he…did he not make it?"

"Oh, no, he's in the ICU." She fiddled with her purse. "He's in an induced coma so we don't know how he is yet. But so far things look okay."

Earl laid his hand across his chest. "Thank God."

"Earl, I came here to meet you and to thank you for saving Jonas's life."

"Oh, you have that backwards, Miss Donna. Jonas saved my life." He explained the final moments on the bus, Jonas insisting that Earl go next because of his family. "But we need him to fight. He didn't seem in a good way during that trip—lost. He needs to fight to live."

Donna nodded, not quite understanding what Earl was referring to. She turned to Jamie. "Is that a tee-ball?"

"Yes! It's my favorite. I saved it from drowning. Lookit what I can do." Jamie frog-hopped the ball from one hand to another.

"You were on the bus, too? Are you okay?"

"Yep. I got to go through the hole in the roof first, and I never touched the water. Earl said I could go first."

Earl interrupted. "Earl said to leave all belongings behind. I don't remember rescuing a ball." He tried to look stern.

Jamie grinned. "I stuffed it in my shirt."

"My nephew Tyler played tee-ball," Donna said softly, watching Jamie toss the ball.

"Jonas's son?"

Donna nodded.

"That explains some things." Earl nodded, thoughtful.

They chatted for a bit, then Donna excused herself after exchanging phone numbers with Lindy and promising to keep them updated.

In the hallway, the hospital's quiet settled back around her. She followed the blue line in reverse, back toward the ICU. Back toward Jonas.

CHAPTER ELEVEN

AFTER A WEEK OF INDUCED COMA, doctors stopped the sedation. Three days later, Jonas woke. His throat was raw, his body weak, but his mind was clear. The neurological tests came back clean—no brain damage from the oxygen deprivation. He'd been lucky.

He told Donna he wanted to live. God had given him a second chance to return to Grace Street. A passion had ignited in him for the kids there—Kyle and the others.

He endured weeks of physical therapy, regaining his strength. Lana called regularly and kept him updated on Grace Street. As he spoke to her on the phone, he'd look at the flower arrangement she'd sent. But his favorite gift was an oversized card colored by the younger children and signed by everyone—a reminder that he was wanted back.

Six weeks later, the doctors cleared him to go home.

His first day back at work, Jonas arrived early. Summer had landed full force while he was gone. After he walked into

Grace Street, he made the rounds turning on the window AC units. The house was perfectly silent except for the humming of lukewarm air being pumped in.

He hadn't been sure how he'd feel once he got here, but a soft peacefulness settled around him. Closing his eyes, he inhaled deeply. Lana's lemon-scent floor cleaner and a whiff of mildew registered. He was home. He smiled and headed to his office.

The front door opened, and Lana blew in. She took one look at Jonas and squealed.

"You're back. You're here. I wasn't expecting you till next week." She rushed over to him and began patting him up and down his arms. "Should you be here already? Is it too soon?" She gripped both of his shoulders.

Jonas chuckled and gave her a quick hug. "I'm back. I'm here. It's not too soon. In fact, I need you to put me to work. I was starting to climb the walls." He continued toward his office with Lana following.

"Well," she said, "you can work, but you are on light duty."

"I don't recall the doctor ordering that."

Lana crossed her arms. "I ordered that. Who do you fear more, me or the doctor?" Her left eyebrow bounced twice, daring him to argue.

He didn't. "Light duty it is."

"I tried to keep up with most of your emails. Counseling appointments won't start till next week. I still have the volunteers scheduled this week to cover for you." She ticked these off on her fingers one by one. "So go into your office, and maybe try to resuscitate that houseplant. I forgot about it. I'm sorry," she said, not sounding sorry.

"Houseplant resuscitation, it is." He smiled with the pure joy of being back and went into his office. He closed the door, encouraging Lana to go about her day. He didn't need a mother hen.

Sitting down at his desk, Jonas looked around. The office was tidy and dustfree. Everything looked perfect except for the pothos on his filing cabinet, withered and crusty. He knew Lana, a woman of remarkable and varied talents, did not have a green thumb.

His desk held only his laptop—recently replaced—and a framed picture of his family. He picked up the photo and stared hard at Kristy, then Tyler. "I miss you guys."

As had happened many times through his recovery, Jonas thought about his encounter in the White. It wasn't a dream or a hallucination from lack of oxygen, as one doctor had suggested. It had been an encounter with God. God hadn't berated him or been disgusted with him. He simply asked Jonas to trust.

Opening the top drawer of his desk, he set the picture in there. It was time to move on.

He was soon busy answering emails and filling up his calendar. At lunchtime, he left his office to help with the lunchline. Lana gave him the eye from across the room, but she was too swamped to act on it. He reacquainted himself with the people coming through. For those who asked, he told them of his miraculous recovery. It felt really good to be back doing what he did best.

By October, he'd settled back into the familiar patterns of Grace Street. The White had changed him, redirected him—of course it had. He could feel it in how confidently he moved through his days now. He was doing God's work. He was fine.

CHAPTER TWELVE

ONE AFTERNOON IN MID-OCTOBER, Kyle showed up.

"How's it going with your dad?" Jonas sat with Kyle on the Grace Street porch. Gingerbread trim and moulding encased the porch. It looked out of place amid the derelict apartment blocks but was spectacular against reds and oranges of the sugar maple tree towering over the house.

"Pretty good. He seems to be sticking around." Kyle sat on the top step, twirling a maple leaf stem with his fingers.

Jonas was comfortably settled in a wicker chair, holding a glass of lemonade. "Were you able to forgive him for leaving you?"

Kyle sighed and tossed the leaf. He leaned back on his elbows. "Not at first. But you were right, I was only hurting myself. Always angry. It was hard, but once I did it, it felt really good, ya know."

Jonas nodded. "That's what grace is—undeserved favor—you don't earn it. The Bible calls it a gift from God. So when you forgave your father, you showed him God's grace." He pointed at Kyle. "You were God's agent on assignment to deliver that grace to your dad. And both of you received the reward for it"

"That's pretty cool."

"It is really cool." Jonas took a swig from his glass.

Kyle didn't say anything for a bit. "That's why Grace Street is called that, huh. Giving this neighborhood what it doesn't deserve."

Jonas chuckled. "Grace Street is here under God's direction to reach out and help his people. You're right—it's not because they earned it, but because he loves them."

Kyle stood up, climbed the last step, and plopped in a chair next to Jonas. "I actually found myself kinda thankful afterward, too."

"How so?"

"None of my friends have dads at home. And that sucks. But I do, so I feel thankful. Even though he isn't the greatest dad ever, he's there now."

"That's amazing insight, Kyle. You should be sure to tell your dad that and also to thank God directly."

Kyle looked at Jonas. "Do you ever have a problem showing grace to someone you really don't like?"

Jonas felt the question like a gut punch. His first instinct was to say "sure" and then redirect the conversation. But this moment felt too big, too important, and as if the question were coming from someone other than Kyle. "Yes, I do struggle with it." He looked out across the street, not actually seeing anything.

Kyle waited.

"You know my family was killed, right?"

Kyle nodded.

"I struggle with forgiving whoever did that."

"Well, there's gotta be limits on the grace thing, doncha think? I mean, forgive a murderer?"

Jonas didn't answer for a long moment. "God doesn't seem to have limits, but it's definitely a human struggle."

"Well, if I ever bump into the creep, I'll take care of him for you." Kyle stood up and shouldered his backpack.

"Vengeance isn't the way, Kyle." Jonas paused. "We have a justice system ordained by God to punish those who take another life. It's not perfect, but that's how we handle this—both as citizens and believers in Christ."

"I guess." Kyle trotted down the steps and raised a hand. "I gotta get home. I'll catch you later."

Jonas sat on the porch for a few more minutes tapping his finger on his knee. Then he got up and headed back into the house—there was always lots to be done.

CHAPTER THIRTEEN

A FEW WEEKS LATER, Jonas helped Lana finish sorting through donations for the clothing closet. The weather was getting colder and people would be in soon looking for warmer clothes.

"I got this." Lana shooed him away. "Last thing I need is you matching and hanging clothes with your colorblindness."

Jonas frowned. "I'm not colorblind."

"Shh. I just gave you an easy out." She began efficiently matching sets together. "It sounds better than the truth that you lack any style sensibility."

Jonas snorted. "It's a donation closet, not a boutique." He headed back to his office. With only an hour left before it was time to head home, he decided to do a quick look through his emails. He opened his laptop and leaned back waiting for it to come online. Only one new email came up. It was from Michael. He clicked on it.

Hello Jonas,

I hope all is well with you. The monthly reports from you and Lana regarding Grace Street have been thorough and encouraging. God is clearly at work!

I mentioned to you—before the accident—a need we have for pastoral care at Dagonport State Correctional Facility. That chaplaincy has been filled, though the candidate we have lined up for it won't start until the beginning of the new year. However, one inmate, Isaiah Jackson, does not have that long. His execution is in two weeks.

You've been cleared to report there on Monday. I'd like you to speak to any death row inmates who request it, but your primary focus is to be on Mr. Jackson. He needs to hear about the love, mercy, and grace of our Lord. The assignment is for one day.

The board of directors and myself will be praying for Mr. Jackson's heart to be open to the truth as you share it with him.

Please send me a brief report following your visit.

Grace and Peace,
Michael

Jonas looked out his office window. The trees were bare now–just one stubborn brown leaf clung to the branch right outside the window, seemingly unaware that its season had passed.

He looked back at his computer screen, fingers ready to hit

reply. Excuses were lining up and falling over one another in his mind. Legitimate excuses. Reasonable objections. Suggestions for alternate solutions that did not include him. His brain quickly sorted through them, discarded some, embellished others. He could make Michael and the board see his logic.

His fingers flying across the keyboard. "Michael, I understand the urgency, but given my recent medical leave and the critical work at Grace Street, I don't think—"

Jonas suddenly stopped. He felt the White fill his mind. It pressed down on the excuses. It supported his flailing will. He felt the vibration still echoing in the space, saying "I've never asked you to understand. Only to trust."

He closed the laptop and lay his head on the desk. Facing the window, he saw that last brown leaf disconnect from its branch in a slight breeze and begin its twirling path downward. It felt so inevitable.

He stood up, packed the laptop away in his satchel, grabbed his coat and headed out.

He passed Lana as she was applying her finishing touches to the donation clothes. "I'm heading home. I won't be in Monday. Michael wants me to head to Dagonport."

Lana searched Jonas's face. "You'll be back on Tuesday?"

He nodded and left.

Early Sunday morning, Jonas rummaged through the donation boxes at Grace Street, pulling out the most battered bibles he could find—worn covers, dog-eared pages, headed for the trash anyway. He stuffed six into his satchel. No point in wasting the nice ones.

Monday morning arrived cold and overcast. Jonas made the drive to Dagonport in silence, radio off, mind carefully blank. He didn't let himself think about what he was driving toward. He just drove.

ACT III

CHAPTER FOURTEEN

ENDLESS LOOPS of razor wire glinted against the belly-bloated clouds; silver spines atop concrete construction framed by a pewter sky—everything sharp, everything gray. Jonas peered through his dirty windshield at the jagged circles flanking the prison grounds, nothing more than a cage for animals. Degenerate beasts unfit for civilization. Monsters.

He put the car in park, grabbed his satchel and got out. A cold wind buffeted him, forcing him to tuck his chin into his collar. It carried the sharp stench of fresh manure from the surrounding fields—something alive and working out there. Here, on an island of black asphalt, just concrete and wire and grim silence.

As he approached the main entrance, sounds began to filter through the wind. A faint metallic hum from the razor wire. The chugging exhaust of a delivery truck idling at a checkpoint.

He opened the door and stepped inside. The manure smell

lingering in his nostrils was replaced by fake-lemon industrial cleaner. Distantly, gates clanged and guards shouted orders.

Navigating his way through the security gauntlet, Jonas removed his keys, phone, wallet, and placed them in a locker. The guards patted him down, waved a wand over his body, and took his satchel. They dumped out the contents—six pocket-sized bibles—and slid the books into a clear plastic bag for him to take. The satchel went into the locker. Even though Michael had gotten prior permission for Jonas to enter as ministerial staff, security was tight.

"You will have a guard with you at all times." A mountain of a man wearing a crisp white shirt with a Dagonport State Correctional Facility patch on the arm motioned for Jonas to step forward and away from the security search area. A badge on his shirt identified him as Doyle. "You will stay on the white line until you reach the cell of the inmate you are here to see." He motioned with a baton to a line that started at his feet and continued down the center of the hall. "You are not to pass anything to inmates other than what has been authorized." He tapped the plastic bag of bibles hanging by Jonas's side. "Understood?"

He nodded.

Doyle turned away and began walking down the white line. Jonas followed. A second burly guard—name tag Foster—stepped up behind them. Muffled shouts echoed. The general inmate population, somewhere else. Everywhere. Even in his head. Gray block walls, the white line, barren. Small black domes along the ceiling, evenly watching. All-seeing eyes.

The plastic bag bounced against Jonas's leg. Disposable bibles for disposable people.

Doyle stopped and pivoted left; Jonas and Foster followed suit. An elevator facing them opened on its own. Stepping inside, they waited. No controls on the wall, no buttons to push. No music. Just the hum of machinery. Brilliant fluorescent lighting bounced off polished silver walls—no space had shadow. Silence pressed down. Finally the doors slid shut, muting the shouts.

The elevator jolted awake. The steel box descended, whirring and clanking. Jonas shifted his plastic bag to the other hand—six bibles, his arsenal. Like descending into an arena to face the lions. He wiped his palm on his pants. Except the lions were caged. He was safe. But his body didn't believe it. After a dozen seconds, the elevator stopped. Metal doors slid open to the belly of the prison. Death row.

As they stepped out, a thick-barred gate blocked the way. Doyle nodded to his right where a brightly lit glassed-in office was tucked in the corner. Several guards within sat at a massive console and bank of monitors. The guardians behind the omniscient domes. Jonas exhaled, his gaze sweeping over the gatekeepers of the zoo.

The guard inside nodded, and with a grating buzz the gate unlocked. They walked through into an open area. The air was heavy and stale—recycled through unseen vents—carrying layers of industrial cleaner, unwashed bodies, and burnt coffee. A suggestion of grease hinted at a meal recently served. Everything smelled locked in.

The glare of caged fluorescents above spotlighted a table.

A few chairs. Beaten-up books stacked on a chair. A chessboard—mid-game—on the table. No windows here in the bowels.

Jonas cleared his throat. "Is this a recreation area for the inmates?"

"Yup," Foster said.

"I didn't think they were allowed out at the same time." He nodded toward the chess game.

"They aren't. Thirty minutes a day out of the cell, one at a time. It takes them weeks to finish a game."

Jonas looked at the chessboard. Weeks. He looked away.

They stopped at the next barred gate. Another hallway stretched beyond. The cells lined one side and faced a blank wall. Thick metal bars fronted the cells with solid walls separating them. The inmates would only see each other when they walked by. Twenty cells lined the hall, though only 13 men awaited execution.

"As interim Chaplain, you are permitted to speak to any inmate you wish. I will accompany you on each stop," Doyle said. Foster walked over to the chessboard and began rearranging pieces. Jonas's jaw tightened. He kept his eyes on Doyle.

Several inmates, peering through their bars at an angle, noticed. They hollered. Raising his voice, Doyle continued, "Stay on the white line until I get the prisoner to move away from his door. Then you may approach. If you wish to pass them a book," he motioned to Jonas's bedraggled selection of bibles, "they go through the meal tray slot. Then step back. Are we clear?"

"Yes." He looked down the long hall of cages. Cages for wild animals. Animals convicted of murder. Murderers he'd been tasked with speaking the truth of God's word to. A total waste of time.

The door buzzed.The three stepped through, the door lock engaging behind them. Foster took a stance at the door. Doyle started the walk down the white line. Jonas followed. "Who do you want to see first?" asked Doyle.

"Isaiah Jackson." And that would be that. In and out.

Clopping of their shoes echoed. Doyle's boots squeaked with each step. Jonas focused on the line, veering neither left nor right. The solid wall to his right, a swath of dingy gray in his peripheral vision, felt safe, supportive. The barred cells opposite left him exposed. He felt eyes on him. Heard murmurs, a low whistle. Predators watching for weakness. His jaw clenched.

"Jackson!" Doyle shouted in the stillness. "You have a visitor." He halted half way down the hall and turned toward a cell. "Chaplain's here to see you. Remain seated on your bed."

Jonas, taking a deep breath, looked into the cell. Just a cage. With a cot-like bed, thin mattress and single blanket. A commode/sink combo. An enclosure to sleep, eat, shit. Exist. A place to mark time until death.

Yet, it was too much. It was larger than the coffins that held his wife and son.

The man sitting on the bed was an older version of the mugshot online. Could have been his father. The young man had hardened and aged. Crew cut, short beard, institutional.

Dragon tattoos still clawed up his neck but had faded over time—pale, shadow dragons.

He looked at Jonas with dead eyes, his gaunt form perched at the edge of the bed. Wary but not curious. Like he wanted to be left alone.

Unrepentant. Of course. No remorse. No shame.

Jonas glanced at Doyle, who nodded, and Jonas stepped forward. "Isaiah, I'm here to give you a copy of the bible if you'd like one."

Isaiah peered at Jonas from the bed. "You a preacher?"

"I'm here as a temporary chaplain."

"But what do you do when you not temporary?"

"I run a ministry in the inner city called Grace Street."

"Grace Street? Weird name. Named for a girl, or somethin'?"

Jonas cleared his throat. "No. Grace has to do with mercy and forgiveness from God. The ministry helps folks having a tough time, with food and clothing, that kind of thing. Do you want the bible I brought?"

Isaiah looked down at the plastic bag by Jonas's side. "You here to give me mercy and forgiveness? You gonna give me *grace?*"

"I'm here to give you God's word." Jonas dug into his bag and pulled out a bible. "Can you read?"

Isaiah nodded.

"I included a bookmark with verses listed for you to contemplate. You can find out what awaits you when you come face-to-face with your Creator." Jonas gripped the tattered book, held it up for Isaiah to see, then smacked it against the tray slot and shoved it through.

Thud.

Good.

Isaiah looked down at the bible on his cell floor, then back up at Jonas. "That's it? You jus' gonna—"

Jonas leaned forward, his breath ghosting the bars. "In ten days you'll suffer the wrath of man," he hissed. "Then you'll face the wrath of God. Justice."

Isaiah jerked back.

Stepping sharply back to the white line, Jonas turned to Doyle. "I'm done here."

The guard raised his eyebrows slightly, but remained silent.

The others would leave him alone now.

Doyle turned to lead Jonas out.

"Yo! Wait up, Bible Man! Can I have one a them?" An inmate several cells down leaned against his bars. An arm stretched out. A finger pointing toward Jonas's plastic bag.

"Me, too!" another echoed.

Doyle glanced at Jonas, who nodded tightly. They approached the cell and stopped, Jonas's feet firmly glued to the white line. "Chaz," the guard called. "Step back and sit on your bed." Chaz complied, and Doyle motioned Jonas forward.

Jonas yanked out another bible. Three steps forward. Tray slot. Shove. *Thud*. He didn't look at Chaz.

Others began to call out. Jonas went through the motions. Three more copies delivered. Each thud of a bible echoed in his skull. He spoke to none of them. He looked at none of them. He waited at the barred door with both guards as it buzzed open. They walked through.

Jonas paused at the chess game—the inmates' recreation. He looked at the board, frozen in time, a battle weeks in the making—patience and strategy on display. His nostrils flared. He wanted to grab the board and throw it across the room. His chest heaved. He needed to get control. He needed to deliver God's message.

Plucked out the last bible. Tossed it on the chessboard. The pieces scattered—plastic rattling against concrete, a queen skittering across the floor. The guards glanced at each other but remained silent. Jonas balled up the bag in his fist.

After retracing his steps through the elevator and halls with the guards, Jonas retrieved his items from the locker—keys, phone, wallet, the things that said he was part of the civilized world; the things that proved he could leave here—and strode out the front door of the building. The prison vomited him out into the parking lot as he rushed towards his car. He got in and collapsed, his forehead pressed against the cold steering wheel. Eyes squeezed shut, tears leaked from the corners.

A haze of memory of himself and Tyler at the dining room table swamped him. *"A pawn moves forward, like this. One space at a time." Jonas nudged the piece, while Tyler bounced in his seat, a gap-toothed grin splitting his face, his small fingers hovering over a piece.*

The image scattered like the chess pieces across the concrete floor. Jonas swiped his hand across his face and started the car. As he drove down the road, he looked in his rearview mirror. Dagonport shrank behind him, its curled razor wire flashing with the dying rays of the sinking sun.

He thanked God he was done with that task.

He never wanted to see that place again.

Michael,

On my visit to Dagonport State Correctional Facilty today, I delivered the Word of God into the hands of the inmate soon-to-be executed, Isaiah Jackson. I also provided him with verse references. He indicated he could read.

Additionally, I provided bibles to several other death row inmates who requested them. I placed a copy in their community room.

The inmates showed little response. The visit was without incident.

Sincerely,
Jonas

CHAPTER FIFTEEN

ISAIAH, still sitting on the bed, stretched out his leg and nudged the bible with his foot. That preacher man—temporary chaplain—whatever, had some nerve. Dude's supposed to save his soul with Sunday School stories, not shove a bible at him and disrespect him with "wrath of man, wrath of God" bullshit. Isaiah considered kicking the bible. Held back though.

He lay down, mumbling, "I'm not an animal in a zoo to throw things at..." He stared at the prison bars that barricaded him in his 6'x9' cell. At least they give zoo animals a tree and sunlight or somethin'.

He rolled over, his face a few inches from the concrete block. "Gram," he whispered. "I ain't no animal." She had taught him that. He remembered her words to him, along with the smell of her kitchen—cinnamon and coffee and acceptance.

But something had gone very wrong.

28 Years Earlier

Minerva Pearl Jackson—Minnie to her friends—sat at her kitchen table, bent over a 1000-piece jigsaw puzzle that was halfway done. A lighthouse on a rocky shoal beneath the summer sun looked back at her. Still missing were the water and sky—the pieces that showed whether the lighthouse faced a storm or calm. The kitchen lighting, a single fixture over the table, wasn't great, so Minnie retrieved a large magnifying glass from her sewing area. That, along with her glasses, made it possible to distinguish the various shades of blue needed to piece them together.

The doorbell rang.

"Good heavens," Minnie glanced at the clock on the stove-top. "It's 9:30. Who's out visitin' after dark?" She set down her magnifying glass and rose from her chair, arthritic joints cracking. Heading for the front door, she patted her hair to make sure it was in order.

Flipping on the porch light, she looked out the peep hole. She gasped, fumbled with the lock, and opened the door. "Tish! What are you doin' here?"

"Hey, Mama. Nice to see you, too." She looked away, tucking a lock of hair behind her ear.

"You're a sight." Minnie looked over her daughter's emaciated form, filthy clothing, and unwashed hair. "Look at me, girl." She gripped Tish's chin, turning her head to face her. "Are you high?"

Tish pushed aside Minnie's hand. "Nah, Ma. I need a small favor. Just for tonight."

"Your pupils are tiny and you got tracks on your arm. You promised me, Tish." Minnie crossed her arms over her chest. Glancing up, she noticed the car idling at the curb. "And you *drove* here like this?"

"Ma. Ma, quit it." Tish scratched at her arm, still not making eye contact. "I didn't drive, Jerome did." She turned and waved toward the car.

"Who's Jerome?"

The back door of the car opened, and 8-year-old Isaiah popped out and walked over. "C'mere Izzy." Tish squatted down and smiled at him. "I need you to stay with Gram tonight. I'll be back tomorrow." She kissed him on the forehead, pushed him toward Minnie, then turned and walked back toward the car.

"Wait! Tish! Where you goin'?" Minnie gathered Isaiah to her, holding him against her side.

Tish never turned around but raised her hand. "Thanks, Ma. Tomorrow!" Isaiah and Minnie watched her get in the car and drive off.

That night Minnie fed the boy and sent him to bathe. She was dismayed at his prominent ribs. A few months ago he seemed fine. She made a bed for him on the couch with fresh-smelling sheets and a comforter, topped with an afghan she'd crocheted.

As Isaiah lay there, officially tucked in, he smiled as Minnie stroked his head. Everything was okay now. He slipped into a deep sleep.

He never saw his mother again.

A few weeks later, life had settled into a new rhythm. Isaiah came home from school and sat at Minnie's kitchen table. "Gram"—cookie crumbs fell from his overstuffed mouth —"the science teacher told us today that we were just animals. Z'at true?"

Minnie dried her hands and looked over at Isaiah. She raised an eyebrow. "Yup, you'd be a pig!" She reached out and rubbed his head, smiling. "Don't talk with your mouth full, young man."

"Yes, ma'am," he mumbled, picking up his glass of milk to wash the cookie down. Minnie pulled out a chair and sat down, waiting as Isaiah grabbed his napkin and wiped his face.

"Good?" He smiled.

"Good. So, science teacher said you're an animal."

"Yep. That we're no different, just evolved more."

"You remember I taught you that God created people," Minnie said.

"Uh huh, and animals and stars and stuff."

"That's right. People *are* similar to animals. It's a good design that works well. But there's a difference," she tapped the table, "and you know what that is?"

"We wear clothes?"

Minnie chuckled. "Yes, we do. But the difference is God gave us something extra."

"What?"

"He made us—all people—image bearers."

Isaiah furrowed his eyebrows. "What's *that* mean?"

"That we were made in the image of God."

"It means we *look* like him?"

"It means that we have been assigned as his representatives on Earth. We have his job of taking care of the Earth and loving one another. Animals don't do that."

"So we're the bosses?" Isaiah sat up straighter.

"We are," Minnie nodded, "but we also have a responsibility to be good bosses. We are to be productive and creative and, above all, kind."

Isaiah nodded.

"And he loves us with a greater love than the animals. He calls us his children. So, no Izzy, in that sense, you are not an animal."

Isaiah jolted awake when the morning buzzer blared and the lights snapped on. No light of dawn or evening dusk arrived here in the death vault under the prison. Just on or off. A light switch in a coffin controlled by someone else.

Five thousand, three hundred days gone. Nine days left.

Time was a strange thing. Every day since he'd been locked up, the days dragged on. There was little to occupy the mind. He'd seen guys go crazy from nothing to do. Each day was monotonous, like counting the bars of his cell over and over, but since there was nothing to set the days apart they scrunched together like an accordion when he looked backwards; he didn't know where the time had gone. Looking forward was like a view of a desert with an indiscernible horizon—nothing to mark the stretch of time or space.

But not now. With his execution pending, time was flying by. Isaiah tried to find things in his mind to grab ahold of the days and slow them down. He fought a constant battle between wanting to be done with it all and go find Gram in Heaven, and his body's instinct to survive regardless of how crappy his life was.

The meal cart clattered down the corridor, wheels squeaking, stopping at each cell to deliver breakfast. He swung his legs over the edge of the bed and got up. Quick splash of water on his face. Sat down at the end of his bed and waited.

He saw the bible on the floor from the day before. Disrespected. His stomach knotted. God had been dead to him for over 20 years, but Gram still lived in his mind. He picked it up–worn pages, bent cover. He set it on the bed. Not touching it. Not yet.

"You gettin' religion now, Isaiah?" Foster slid a breakfast tray through the slot. "Good timing since you'll be meetin' God, oh, sometime next week." He chuckled and walked away.

After Isaiah had eaten, he dropped to the narrow space next to his bed and did pushups. Rep after rep after rep. Treated like an animal. But Gram— He pushed harder. Muscles burning. She loved God. Isaiah had loved her. He crashed down, his muscles rebelling. Dragged himself up onto the bed.

Something about that bible just kept on grabbing at him.

He slid the bible across the blanket. His Gram had a nice fake-leather one, filled with her underlining and notes. Not this one, but he supposed the words would be the same. Gram's words.

He tugged at the bookmark sticking out the top a bit. Isaiah didn't know where anything was in the bible—he'd always just listened to Gram talk about it—so the verses listed by the preacher guy were as good a place to start as any.

Half a dozen references were scrawled in a column. Isaiah squinted. Messy handwriting. Someone musta been in a hurry...or angry. The letters stabbed into the paper. The first one looked to say Matthew. Isaiah flipped to the table of contents, and ran his finger down the list of books till he found Matthew. He turned to that page number, then a few more to get to the right chapter and verse.

Never a great reader, he had to read out loud, but he kept his voice low.

"Then he will say to those on his left, 'Depart from me, you cursed, into the eternal fire prepared for the devil and his angels."

Sounded just like the angry preacher. Nothing like Gram. He turned to the next verse listed, also in Matthew.

"So it will be at the end of the age. The angels will come out and separate the evil from the righteous and throw them into the fiery furnace. In that place there will be weeping and gnashing of teeth."

Isaiah shifted on the bed and began chewing his lower lip. Maybe Matthew was an angry preacher too. He looked at the next reference on the bookmark. Thessa-something. He flipped back to the table of contents and got the page number, another one near the back of the bible. Finding the chapter and verse, he read:

"...when the Lord Jesus is revealed from heaven with his mighty angels in flaming fire, inflicting vengeance on those who do not know God and on those who do not obey the gospel of our Lord Jesus. They will suffer the punishment of eternal destruction..."

Isaiah repeated, his lips mouthing the words. "*...those who do not obey...Will suffer the punishment of eternal destruction—*"

He tossed the book aside. Damn. That did not sound like the place of no pain Gram talked about. He scrubbed his hands across his face and through his hair. Fisted them yanking on the short strands. Why hadn't she mentioned these words? He slumped. Because she was good and expected he would be too.

But he wasn't.

Isaiah jumped up. Paced back and forth like a caged animal. Hunted. Exposed. His past. Crimes. Guilt cascaded down on him. Grabbed the bars and banged his head. Stop!

"You okay over there, Izzy?" Mac asked.

"Goin' to hell." Isaiah spoke quietly, his voice cracking.

"Aren't we all. Aren't we all..."

"No. For real, Mac. Forever." He sat back on his bed. "Next week..." He picked up the bookmark. Maybe there were good verses, too. The joy of the Lord. All that stuff Gram talked about. The last three references were in the same book: Revelation. The table of contents directed him to the end of the bible. The last book.

"I can hear you mumbling over there. Read a little louder so I can hear what you're saying," Mac said.

"Yeah," someone farther down spoke up. "Read to us, Izzy!"

Why not? Why not read loud enough so all the guys could hear. Nothin' left to lose.

Isaiah cleared his throat and read the first passage: *"And if anyone's name was not found written in the book of life, he was thrown into the lake of fire."*

"Say what?" "Damn." Nervous laughter from someone. Isaiah kept reading.

"...he also will drink the wine of God's wrath, poured full strength into the cup of his anger, and he will be tormented with fire and sulfur in the presence of the holy angels and in the presence of the Lamb."

He stumbled over some of the words, throat tight. Had to keep clearing it. But the hall had fallen silent.

"Keep going, Izzy. You're doing good," Mac said.

"But as for the cowardly, the faithless, the detestable, as for murderers, the sexually immoral, sorcerers, idolaters, and all liars, their portion will be in the lake that burns with fire and sulfur, which is the second death."

Isaiah's voice stopped. He grabbed his hair again. "Murderers, murderers," he repeated till he fell over sideways sobbing. He didn't notice the total silence that had fallen over the cell block. Twelve other men witnessing him falling apart. All of them hearing their own names in that list.

24 Years Earlier

Isaiah sat hunched in a hard plastic chair, every nerve in his body a live wire. The rhythmic blip of the heart monitor ratcheted up the fear screaming in his brain. He rubbed a hand across his eyes to swipe away the leaking tears. But they kept coming.

Who could do such a thing? He glanced up at Gram stretched out on the hospital bed, face ashen in the glare of the fluorescent light bar mounted on the wall. Ashen except where purple bruises bloomed around her eyes. Stitches zigzagged across her forehead and her bottom lip had a thick brown crust where it'd been split open. Looked small and weak and dead.

Isaiah looked at her chest to make sure it was still moving up and down, the heart monitor not enough to reassure him. He reached out and covered her hand with his. So cold. He pulled the sheet overtop, keeping a gentle grip on it. He looked out the window.

Leaden clouds, bloated and still, filled his view as sleet began to ping off the glass. If sadness were a color, he was looking at it.

"Izzy?" Minnie's scratchy, barely there voice drew Isaiah's attention from the window.

He jumped up and leaned over her, still holding her hand. "Gram, you're awake!" Relief washed through him.

"Young man, those tears I see better not be for me."

"Nah." Isaiah rubbed the sleeve of his free arm across his face. "Allergies."

Minnie smiled. "Scooch yer chair closer. Sit down" His

chair scraped across the linoleum and he sat, never letting go of her hand. “When the doc came in earlier, he said you were in the waiting room talking to a lady from the state. What happened?”

“Nothin’ much. She smelled funny.”

She chuckled, then coughed. “What did she say?”

“Said they couldn't find my mom or dad, so gonna put me with a family till you got outta here. But I told her that wasn't happenin’, that I'd stay here with you till you were better.” Isaiah chewed his lower lip. "Gram, who did this to you?"

"Oh, just some young men. Tried to take my purse. I wouldn't let go." She shifted in the bed. "It was stupid of me to hang on. Stubborn, I suppose."

"They should be locked up forever."

"Oh Izzy, they're just lost boys who need help..." Minnie sighed. “What did the social worker say next?”

“She said I wasn't allowed to stay here, but I'm not lettin’ them take me away to no other family. You *are* my family.”

“Izzy.”

A muffled announcement came over the speaker in the hallway, then everything went quiet, except the blipping monitor and sleet brushing against the window in earnest now.

“Izzy,” she repeated softly. “The doc said those fellows who mugged me did a lot of damage. They need to operate but my heart is too weak—”

“No!” Isaiah jumped up. “No, you are not gonna die. You can't leave me, Gram.” He was shaking. Tears dripped down his cheeks.

"Sit down and listen to me, boy." She squeezed his hand. "Even if I die here, now, it isn't really dying. It's more like movin'. I'll be movin' to a much better place. No pain. No muggers." She flicked her eyes toward the window. "No sleet."

"Gram, I know but not yet. I still need you here."

"That's not my call, it's up to the Lord." Her voice was getting quieter. "But I'll be waitin' for you, Izzy. One day we'll be in paradise together. Just imagine!"

Isaiah sobbed, snot running down his face, gasping for air between wails. He didn't care who heard him in the hallway. Gram was dyin'. He couldn't stop it.

"Hush, my boy. We won't meet up just yet." She closed her eyes. "You're gonna grow up to be a man, one who is kind and lovin'. You'll be brave. And above all you will trust in all I've taught you."

Social services came later that day and made Isaiah leave Minnie's side. He argued. Begged. Lashed out. Hospital security escorted him to the stinky woman's car, and she silently drove him to his new "family." Gram died overnight. Isaiah wasn't there for her.

Isaiah lay on the concrete floor of his cell, the memory of Gram's hospital room fading. The sleet. The beeping monitor. Her cold hand.

She'd asked him to be kind. Loving. Brave.

He'd become a murderer, just like the "lost boys" who killed her.

And in nine days, he'd face the same God she'd gone to meet.

The same God whose wrath the angry preacher promised was waiting.

Isaiah curled into himself, shaking. There was no way out. No way to undo what he'd done. No way to become the man Gram believed he could be.

He was exactly what that preacher said. Cursed. Destined for hell—not just a few minutes in an execution chamber, but forever.

Then somewhere, deep in the back of his mind, Gram's voice whispered something else. A story. About a son who came home...

"Izzy...Izzy!" Mac whisper-called out. "Man, you okay?"

Isaiah rolled onto his stomach and propped himself up on his arms. "Mac?" His voice came out much louder than he'd intended. Wobbly. He realized he didn't care if the other guys overheard him. His pride had shattered, its cold shards scattered beyond gathering. He felt like an exposed wound.

"D'jou go to Sunday School, Mac?"

"Yeah, sure."

"You remember a story about a boy, left home with his pops' money, spent it all. He was poor and hungry, didn't want to eat pig food or something, so he went home. Pops was happy to see him. I can't remember what happened next. You know that one?"

"It sounds familiar. I remember his older brother was a dick."

"Prodigal Son." echoed from farther down the cell block.

"Prodigal Son," Isaiah repeated. "Yeah, I think that's right. You know where that's at in the Bible, Chaz?"

"Nah. Ask Doyle. He'll look it up for you."

Isaiah sat up, wiping his face with his sleeve. His hands shook, but something—some small thread of hope—was tugging him forward.

CHAPTER SIXTEEN

THE SHARP BUZZER and bright light woke Isaiah. He moved through his morning routine quicker than usual. Hellfire had followed him into his dreams the night before. He was in a burning house. Trapped. Chunks of ceiling falling around him. Thick smoke choking and bright orange embers raining down. A wall collapsed, pinning him. Flames raced in. Paralyzed with terror, Isaiah screamed. But through that all, deep in his mind, he heard his gram whispering. "Hush, my boy. There is still hope..."

Isaiah gulped down a few handfuls of water from the sink. Splashed some on his face. When he heard the meal cart squeaking down the hallway, he quickly dried his hands and face. He strode to the bars to see if Doyle was on duty.

It was indeed Doyle, just arriving at his cell.

"Back up, Jackson. You know the drill."

Isaiah stepped back and sat on his bed. "Doyle, can I ask you something?"

Doyle raised an eyebrow as he set the tray down on the pass through. “Yeah, go ahead.”

"You know the Bible?"

"My mom made me go to church. Why?"

"There's a story. Prodigal Son. You know where that is?"

Doyle frowned. "That's the one where the kid comes home and the dad throws a party, right?"

"Yeah."

"I remember the story. Don't know where it is though." He paused, looking at Isaiah's face. "You need to find it?"

"Yeah."

Doyle shifted his weight, glanced back toward the control room. "Yeah, okay. I'll look it up and tell you at tray pickup."

Doyle walked away. Isaiah sat on his bed, tray untouched, Bible clutched in his hand, waiting.

Fifteen minutes felt like an hour.

Doyle came back. "Luke 15, starting at verse 11."

Isaiah looked up. "Luke 15:11. Thanks, man."

Doyle lingered for a second. "My mom used to say that was her favorite story."

"Why?"

"She said everyone needs to know they can come home." Doyle cleared his throat, shifted his stance. "Anyway. You need anything else?"

"Nah. This is good. Thanks."

Doyle walked away, but something in his expression had changed.

“I'm bored, Izzy. Read it good and loud,” Chaz said.

"Yeah, yeah, hold on a sec." Isaiah's finger skimmed down the list of books. "Luke, Luke, Luke...," he whispered. "Luke!" He flipped to the starting page. "Shit. Which chapter?"

Three inmates chorused back, "Fifteen!"

"Got it." Isaiah sat down on the floor. Leaned against the bars. Cleared his throat.

"There was a man who had two sons. And the younger of them said to his father, 'Father, give me the share of property that is coming to me.' And he divided his property between them. Not many days later, the younger son gathered all he had and took a journey into a far country, and there he squandered his property in reckless living—"

"Yeah, whorin' and gamblin', whoop!"

"Shut up. Let him read."

"And when he had spent everything, a severe famine arose in that country, and he began to be in need. So he went and hired himself out to one of the citizens of that country, who sent him into his fields to feed pigs. And he was longing to be fed with the pods that the pigs ate, and no one gave him anything—"

Snort. "Pig pods be prison food!"

"Shut up!" chorused down the hall.

"But when he came to himself, he said, 'How many of my father's hired servants have more than enough bread, but I perish here with hunger! I will arise and go to my father, and I will say to him, 'Father, I have sinned against heaven and before you. I am no longer worthy to be called your son. Treat me as one of your hired servants.'

"And he arose and came to his father. But while he was still a long way off, his father saw him and felt compassion, and ran and embraced him and kissed him. And the son said to him, 'Father, I have sinned

against heaven and before you. I am no longer worthy to be called your son—'"

"My father told me I was a mistake. This some fairy tale shit."

"Yeah, Martinez, your old man was wrong," Mac said. "Keep going, Izzy."

"But the father said to his servants, 'Bring quickly the best robe, and put it on him, and put a ring on his hand, and shoes on his feet. And bring the fattened calf and kill it, and let us eat and celebrate. For this my son was dead, and is alive again; he was lost, and is found.' And they began to celebrate."

Isaiah's voice cracked on the last words. He lowered the Bible to his lap. Stared at it.

"Dead and is alive again," he whispered. "Was lost, and is found."

He looked up at the cinderblock wall across from him, seeing nothing. Gram had been right. There was a way home.

For a long moment, no one spoke.

"Man, that's just a story," someone muttered.

"Nah." Mac's voice was firm. "Nah, I remember that one now. My ma told it different, but... same ending. The dad just takes him back. No questions."

"No questions?" Isaiah looked at the passage again. Mac was right. Dude never got to the part about coming back as a servant—robe, ring, sandals, feast, wasn't no servant. "He didn't even let him finish..."

"No real dad does this." Martinez sneered.

"You're right, most dads wouldn't." Mac said. "I wouldn't if it'd been my kid. But Ma told me it was a parable, kinda like a picture."

Isaiah's voice cracked. "The dad just... he ran *to* him. Didn't wait for him to apologize right or nothin'. Just—" He couldn't finish. The sobs choked off his words.

Mac's voice came quiet from the next cell: "Ma said that's what God's like. For real."

"Jonas, welcome!" Michael smiled and motioned him forward. "Please come in and have a seat."

Jonas nodded to the assembled group of eight as he walked around the table to the only vacant seat and sat down.

Michael continued. "I think you've met everyone here at one time or another over the years."

"Yes, it's good to see you all again." Jonas forced a smile as he looked around at the board of directors of Grace Ministry, the bureaucratic oversight to various ministries throughout the region. A necessary evil in Jonas's eyes.

"Last time the board convened, several members had specific questions about Grace Street, and I thought no one could answer them better than you. Hence your requested presence to join us today."

"Certainly," Jonas leaned his elbows on the table and folded his hands. "It's my passion. I'm happy to talk your ear off about it."

A few members chuckled.

"Splendid!" Michael turned to an older woman on his left. "Mrs. Kistler, would you like to start us off?"

"Yes, thank you." Mrs. Kistler turned toward Jonas. "Jonas, we love the work you do with those poor souls downtown. Do you feel that you and your employees are safe there?"

"Safe?"

"Well, yes. It's not a very nice part of town, and the street people and addicts...well, you know. They can be dirty and dangerous. And the language they use, goodness! I just don't want to think you are in harm's way."

Jonas looked over at Michael as if to say, is she for real? Michael smiled at Jonas and lifted an eyebrow.

Jonas cleared his throat. "Uh, yes, Mrs. Kistler. I feel that we take adequate safety precautions at our facility. We try not to focus on the dirt and language and just provide for the local people's most pressing needs."

"Oh, good! I had an idea I wanted to run by you." She lowered her head like she had a secret she was excited to share. "Christmas isn't too far off, so I thought if you decorated the building—Christmas trees, ornaments, tinsel, lights, the works—" her face had completely lit up. "A Santa so those disadvantaged children could sit on his lap, and a photographer there offering portraits, at a reasonable price—"

"Mrs. Kistler," Jonas scrambled through his brain for a tactful reply. "I think that is a lovely idea, but that would definitely present us with possibly some firecode issues and definitely security concerns."

"Oh." Her expression fell. "Oh, I wasn't thinking. Of course, you're right."

"I'll tell you what, though." Jonas smiled kindly. "We hold a Christmas Eve service open to the public. Lana plays the piano and we sing carols, serve hot chocolate, that kind of thing, and you could join us."

Mrs. Kistler nodded. "Thank you, Jonas." She didn't look like she'd be coming anywhere near the place.

Jonas looked back at Michael who gave him a small nod and conspiratorial smile.

"Mr. Duncan." Michael motioned to the man across from Jonas. "I believe you were the other one with a question?"

"Yes," Mr. Duncan cleared his throat and tapped a sheaf of papers on the table. "My concern, as treasurer, is the proportion of our budget going to Grace Street in terms of money invested versus results, and if those two are being balanced responsibly. Can you support or justify the somewhat high expenditures?"

Jonas frowned. "This isn't the kind of work that produces quantifiable results. It can't be measured that way." He shifted in his chair to look around the table. "We are reaching the poor, the discouraged, the youth, and, yes, the addicted and homeless. We give them food, clothes, and hope." Jonas tapped the table. "We demonstrate unconditional love and teach them that, no matter their circumstances, they aren't beyond God's reach—that no one is!"

The words rang hollow in his own ears. He'd just told a man he was damned to hell. Grace for the deserving. Justice for— Jonas cleared his throat.

"You can't assign a price tag to that."

Mr. Duncan leaned back, arms crossed. "I'm just saying,

Jonas, we need accountability. How do we know these people aren't taking advantage?"

Jonas kept his voice steady. "Because grace isn't about deserving. We help because they're made in God's image."

"Even the ones who won't help themselves?"

"Especially them."

"Ah, but as noble as that sounds, we have a fiduciary responsibility to our donors to spend their donations wisely."

Jonas clamped his mouth shut.

Michael intervened. "Jonas has been given a budget, and I think he has done an exemplary job of staying within those constraints. Maybe you could look through the line items and bring any specific expenditures to the board's attention at a future meeting."

Jonas exhaled.

Michael turned to him. "I really liked what you said about no one being beyond God's reach. That's powerful. That is love in action and deed." To the rest of the members, he said, "And that is what true grace is all about!"

Everyone murmured agreement.

He turned back to Jonas. "Earlier this week, I asked you to go to death row at Dagonport. Your brief report indicated you didn't feel the inmates were particularly receptive to God's message of hope."

"Murderers and child molesters, Michael." Mrs. Kistler shuddered.

Michael kept his gaze pinned to Jonas. "Do you think murderers are beyond God's reach?"

Jonas cleared his throat. He had to look away from

Michael's searching gaze. "No, of course not. He is all powerful and can perform miracles. I simply indicated I didn't see any signs of the Spirit at work there."

Jonas felt the hypocrisy sitting in his chest like a stone. Grace for the acceptable poor. Not for—

He shut the thought down. That was different. Those men deserved exactly what they were getting.

"Thank you, Jonas."

CHAPTER SEVENTEEN

"HEY, MAC." Isaiah leaned against his bars. "You there?"

Mac snorted. "Sure, dude. Six years now."

"Yeah, yeah, I meant—"

"What's on your mind, Izzy?"

"I looked up that verse again. First one on the book mark. Guess what?"

"What?"

Isaiah slid down to the floor and set the Bible on his knees. "Preacher gave me '*Depart from me, you cursed, into eternal fire*'—BUT right above it..." He moved his finger up over the words. "Here. It says. *'Come, you who are blessed by my Father, inherit the kingdom prepared for you from the foundation of the world.'* Ya hear that, Mac? A good verse right by the bad verse."

Mac whooshed out a breath. "Yeah, I hear that. Talkin' about the Father again.

Try another one...see if it's got a good verse, too."

"Give it to me." Chaz called out. "I got a bible. I'll look it up."

He gave him the next verse in Matthew. Then, one by one, the other inmates who'd received bibles from Jonas asked for a verse. Isaiah gave them the references.

"Anyone else?" he called out. "I got one more."

The loudspeaker came on overhead. "Yeah, Jackson. I'll take it."

"That you, Doyle?" Mac asked.

"Yeah, it's me. Give me your last verse, Jackson. We'll look it up."

Isaiah's grin widened. He shouted out the last verse.

"Okay everybody, look for a good verse near the one I gave you."

After some paper rustling, the men found their references and skimmed a little before and a little after. "Got it!" rang out through the cell block.

"Yo, Chaz. You're up first. Bad then good."

"It says '*and throw them into the fiery furnace. In that place there will be weeping and gnashing of teeth—*'" Chaz knocked on the bars. "Listen to this. It also says '*the righteous will shine like the sun in the kingdom of their* Father.'"

Silence.

"But we ain't righteous." The comment hung there.

Mac's voice came quiet. "Remember the prodigal son. Dude was a total loser. But he came back home, returned to his father. That must be what makes someone righteous..."

Martinez continued. "Mine's got '*eternal destruction*'—but also '*God will give relief to those who are afflicted!*' Relief, man!"

"I got the next one," said Bronsky. "*Tormented with fire and sulfur*—but '*Blessed are the dead who die in the Lord from now on... that they may rest!*'"

"Rest and relief sound good about now," Isaiah whispered.

Mitch was next up. "Guys. You gotta listen to this one..."*The wages of sin is death*—" his voice cracked "—*but the gift of God is eternal life!*"

The cell block fell silent.

Then, quietly, from somewhere down the line: "Damn."

"Doyle, you're up man," Mac called. "You find one?"

A pause. The loudspeaker clicked on.

Then sounding as if God himself was booming from Heaven above:

"It is done! I am the Alpha and the Omega, the beginning and the end. To the thirsty I will give from the spring of the water of life without payment. The one who conquers will have this heritage, and I will be his God and he will be my son."

Silence settled again.

Isaiah leaned his head back against the bars, tears streaming down his face.

"Father, I want to come home."

ACT IV

CHAPTER EIGHTEEN

JONAS AND LANA sat in his office, gripping mugs of hot coffee to ward off the chill. Winter waited in the wings, sending heralds of cold, gusty winds to announce its imminent arrival. The Victorian home that housed Grace Street was a beautiful reminder of an earlier time of architectural imagination—high ceilings, intricately designed moldings, alcoves in surprising places.

But it was drafty. Jonas's office had a fireplace. It was no longer up to code, so he'd set an electric radiator in it to boost the temperature of the room. They had just finished reviewing the schedule for the upcoming month—day-to-day operations, meal plans, and special events.

Lana leaned back in her chair, sipping the hot coffee. "Oh! Did you see the local news this morning?"

"No. What's going on?"

"Dagonport—that inmate you went to see. What was his name?"

"Isaiah Jackson."

"Right. His execution is scheduled for midnight tonight—"

Jonas nodded. Finally justice would be served. The wheels had turned slowly—fifteen years—but the day of reckoning had arrived.

"—but there has been a huge development." Lana sipped her coffee.

"What do you mean?"

Lana leaned forward. "I think that you, Jonas, have been used by God to create a miracle." She smiled. "Someone has filed a stay of execution with the governor."

Jonas shook his head and sighed. "That's not uncommon. Either nothing comes of it, or the execution—and justice—gets postponed a bit."

"No, you don't understand. The media was all abuzz about a revival that has broken out on death row. Not just Isaiah, but other inmates, as well! I think your visit there was the catalyst to hearts changed—and very tough hearts at that."

Jonas froze.

She continued, beaming broadly now. "I am so proud of you, Jonas. Your obedience to God has led these men to salvation!"

He set his coffee down on the desk before he spilled it. "If revival has come to death row, it wasn't me. That was all God." He couldn't bring himself to look up and see the misplaced respect he knew would be shining from Lana's eyes.

Lana got up and walked around the desk. She gave Jonas a side hug. "You are so humble. Of course the power came from the Lord, but he used *you* to deliver it." She looked at him for a beat, but he couldn't move or speak. "Hey, I know this has been tough because of Kristy and Tyler. But you rose above that. You are a good man, Jonas." She gave him a peck on top of his head and left the room.

Jonas exhaled when his door clicked shut. He couldn't process any thoughts because his mind was awash in red coals.

After a bit, he shook his head to dislodge the sensations coursing through him. It was garbage. Complete and utter garbage. Revival was the claim of desperation of a man headed for execution followed by eternal damnation.

He had work to do. He pulled his laptop forward and opened it, waiting for his email program to load. He clicked on the first message; it was from Michael.

Jonas,

I'm sure you've heard about the remarkable events at Dagonport. Isaiah Jackson's execution is scheduled for tonight at midnight, but there's been a stay request filed on his behalf.

Regardless of the outcome, something profound has happened on death row.

I'm driving out this evening to attend the prayer vigil which begins at 7pm. I thought you might want to be there as well—to witness what God has done through your obedience and to rejoice in the grace he's shown to these men.

If you'd like to meet, I'll be in the parking lot near the main entrance.

Grace and peace,
Michael

Jonas stared at the email for a long time. Clearly, Michael believed the revival was real. And also just as clearly, Jonas was expected to be there. He could probably fake being joyous about a revival he didn't believe had actually happened. The deception sat askew in his gut, a blocky weight with sharp corners jabbing at unexpected angles, but he'd been given no choice. All of this would resolve at midnight—or whenever they finally carried out the inevitable.

He began to pack up his work for the day as it now appeared he'd be leaving soon to travel to Dagonport. He felt a dark satisfaction—he'd be there to witness the ending of Isaiah Jackson, killer of innocent people.

He paused as a new thought filtered across his mind. What if revival really had happened? What if Jackson had somehow become *saved*? God knew it wasn't through Jonas's effort, but still... Jonas gripped his face with his hand, squeezing his eyes. This would be so typical of God. Extending grace to the worst of the worst. He dragged his hand down his face.

Standing up, he grabbed his coat and satchel. Whatever. He just needed this day to be over. He needed this distraction to go away so he could get back to doing the Lord's work.

The sun set as Jonas drove toward Dagonport. The orange globe sank out of view in his rearview mirror. The evening would be clear and cold. As he drove, he knew he should be talking to God—hashing out his feelings and receiving guidance in reorienting his thought processes—but he kept himself locked down instead.

He signaled and exited the highway. Dagonport was still one exit farther along, but Jonas wanted to grab some dinner and, if he were being honest with himself, some mental prep time before the evening. He turned into the parking lot of a diner and parked near the back by a dumpster. He noticed his choice—tucked away, out of sight—but didn't examine it further.

Inside, he requested a booth near the back. The gum-snapping waitress led him there and handed him a menu. "The special tonight is meatloaf and mashed potatoes. Can I get you something to drink?"

"Yes, I'll have coffee, and the special sounds perfect." He handed back the menu, and she left.

After he took off his coat and got settled, he looked up and noticed a TV hanging in the corner of the room just a few booths away. The sound was muted, but he recognized the curling razorwire of Dagonport.

The waitress returned with his coffee and a bowl of creamer cups.

"Since there aren't many people here, would you mind turning on the sound for the TV?" he asked her.

"Sure thing, honey." She walked over to the counter, picked up a remote and aimed it at the screen.

The reporter on the screen was bundled against the cold, her cheeks and nose pink as if she'd been outside for a while. She stood in a parking lot with a corner of Dagonport's gray wall over one shoulder and the razorwire-topped fence stretching behind her out of frame. Huge sodium lamps in the parking lot lit the scene, with brighter white spotlights atop the fencing behind.

"—Yeah, Rick, we've been here at Dagonport State Correctional Facility for a while now watching people arrive. Of course, tonight at midnight Isaiah Jackson is scheduled to be executed. We are waiting for the moment that word comes from the governor's office as to his decision on the stay of execution. The stay was not filed by Jackson's attorney, but it is unclear who did file it.

"To my left is a large group of people assembling—" The camera panned to the right showing dozens of people clumped together, holding signs. "—Many are here in defense of the victims' family and looking for justice to be served. I've also had word that a prayer vigil is scheduled to begin soon." The camera panned back to the reporter, then to the left, showing a smaller group of people standing together and talking. The camera came back to the reporter. "I have with me one of the prison guards from the death row cell block." She motioned, and he stepped into frame.

The waitress set Jonas's dinner on the table. He thanked her.

The reporter turned to the man. "This is Patrick Doyle. Thank you for speaking to us. I know you were leaving work, headed home."

"Yes, ma'am."

"We've heard rumors of a revival that spread through death row, and that is what prompted the filing of the stay of execution. Can you comment on that? Have you seen evidence of it?"

"Yes, I can. And I've definitely seen it with my own eyes. In fact, the revival has included some of the guards." Doyle smiled broadly. "I'm a new man."

The reporter paused, as if she hadn't been expecting this twist to the story. "Can you tell us how it began?"

"Sure thing. A chaplain came to the block, specifically to see Jackson. He handed out some bibles."

Jonas cringed. The memory of throwing the bible across the chessboard and watching the pieces scatter flitted across his mind.

Doyle continued. "The inmates began sharing verses with each other. Impromptu Bible studies popped up. They included the guards in their conversation. There was singing! The Lord moved mountains and hearts changed. Praise God!"

"Do you think Isaiah Jackson is a genuinely changed man, repentant of his crimes?"

"Yes, ma'am, I do think so. It's not unusual for inmates scheduled for execution to suddenly find God—no atheists in foxholes and all that—and it's not my place to judge one way or the other if it's real. But often they are also fighting the execution. Jackson is different. I don't think he wants to die, but he seems at peace with it. He has a greater purpose in God's kingdom. The Lord has forgiven his sins, but Jackson also realizes there are consequences to his crimes and, I dunno, he just seems at peace with it."

"Do you think he deserves to have his death sentence commuted to life?"

"That's not my place to say."

"Thank you, Patrick, for speaking with us." Doyle walked away and the reporter faced the camera.

Jonas slowly shook his head, looking out the window. It had become a mirror as darkness set in. He looked at himself and looked away again. He knew the power of God's word. That was why he never wanted to go to Dagonport in the first place. God could save Isaiah's soul—Jonas had known that all along. He just didn't want him to.

Isaiah had stolen a mother's life. A child's life. They had no choice, no future, no chance. And family left behind? Left to pick up pieces that could never be put back together.

Where was their justice?

The reporter continued. "We spoke to the husband and father of the victims earlier. He is here tonight—but interestingly he is attending the prayer vigil, not the protest. He said," she glanced down at her notes fluttering in her gloved hand, "that he is 'thrilled to hear about Isaiah's repentance,' that he 'had been praying for him for fifteen years,' and that he 'has forgiven him.'"

Jonas slammed his hand down on the table.

The waitress came rushing over. "Is anything wrong? Would you like something instead of the meatloaf?"

Jonas apologized. "Could you please put this in a to-go box for me. I just wasn't as hungry as I thought."

While she left to pack his dinner, he yanked some bills out of his wallet and tossed them on the table. He stuffed his arms into his coat sleeves. He wasn't even sure who he was angry at. But he was boiling mad.

Jonas headed out to the parking lot, styrofoam to-go container in hand. Arriving at his car, he set the container on the roof and dug into his pocket for his keys. Now that it was fully dark, he felt exposed under the parking lot light that shone down on him like a spotlight.

As he clicked the button on his key fob, he heard rustling. He spun around. Tracking his eyes along the dumpster behind him, Jonas searched for the source of the noise. There it was again, near the back—a scuffling. He slowly approached. The back end and swooping tail of a puppy jutted out from behind the dumpster.

Jonas squatted and whistled. The tail disappeared, but a moment later, a nose poked back around. "Come here, boy." Jonas patted his thigh. "What are you doing back there?" It was difficult to see the dog in the shadow.

"I won't hurt you," Jonas cooed. The dog emerged from behind the dumpster and approached him cautiously. He reached his hand out and the puppy nuzzled into it. "Aw, you're friendly." The dog wagged its tail, while Jonas rubbed his head and stroked down his body. Knobs of spine protruded along the top and swept down into a prominent rib cage. "Come here in the light where I can see you."

Shifting back so the dog was out of the shadow, Jonas gasped. It was a black lab, a few months old. It had a white patch on top of its head, vaguely heart-shaped. "Oh, dear

Lord. You look just like Kiki when she was a puppy," he whispered.

The dog wagged its tail again.

Jonas did a quick visual inspection. "You are way too thin, and you are a girl, my apologies." He smiled as tears gathered in his eyes. The puppy licked Jonas's face. "Oh, sweetheart."

He stood up and looked around the parking lot to see if anyone could be missing their dog, but no one was outside. Removing his jacket, he squatted down. Wrapped her body in the warm fabric. Hugged her to his body and stood up. She stared into his eyes, completely trusting him. "How about you hang out with me for a bit, until we figure out what's what." He opened the car door and set her on the passenger seat, still wrapped in his coat. He grabbed the styrofoam container and slid into the driver's seat.

He started the car and turned up the heat. The dog sniffed the air, snout pointed toward the food on Jonas's lap. "You hungry?" She barked once. Jonas pet her again, marveling at the heart shape on her head. "Can I call you Kiki for now? We can come up with a new name later, but you remind me of my Kiki." She thumped her tail against the seat.

Jonas carefully opened the container, the aroma of meatloaf and mashed potatoes filling the car. "Let's see what you think of the house special."

Kiki thought the house special was just fine and finished it in a few bites, licking up every bit of gravy. Taking a bottle of water from the console, Jonas poured some into the styrofoam container. Kiki lapped that up. When she was done, she turned several circles and lay down on the seat, her head propped on Jonas's leg. She watched his face as he adjusted his coat to cover her again.

They sat in silence for a while, Jonas petting her as she fought to keep her eyes open. "Hey, sweetheart," he whispered. "There's somewhere I need to be. I sure could use the company. What do you think?" She licked his hand, then closed her eyes.

Jonas gently repositioned her head from his leg to her seat, started the car, and pulled out of the parking lot.

CHAPTER NINETEEN

At the on-ramp, he paused. The highway stretched ahead, and just beyond—maybe two miles—the sky glowed orange with Dagonport's lights.

We'll leave the light on for you—the Motel 6 slogan drifted across his mind. He snorted. *Roaches check in, but they don't check out*. Yeah. That was more like it.

He could turn around. Go home. Kiki stirred in her sleep.

He pulled onto the highway, heading toward that glow.

He took the exit, then turned onto the access road to the prison, its white center line glowing under the bright lights. The parking lot was more active now than it had looked on the news. On one side was a rowdy crowd, shouting, with picket signs jabbing the air. On the other, a smaller group stood in a semicircle holding candles, shoulders hunched. Bridging the two was a phalanx of media vans topped with satellite dishes. It resembled a modern-day gallows scene with all the townsfolk assembled, anxious for a hanging.

Jonas backed into a space a short distance away, but with

all three groups in view. He put the car in park, leaving it running for the heat. Kiki slept soundly, her back foot rhythmically kicking like she was running in her dream. He reached over and traced the white heart shape on her head.

"Dad, we need to pick this one!" Tyler sat on the floor at the animal shelter, surrounded by a litter of puppies crawling over him. He held one squirming puppy aloft. "The heart on her head is special. It means God chose her for us." How could Jonas say no to that reasoning? Kiki came home with them that day. A gift from God.

Leaning over to the new-Kiki, Jonas kissed her forehead. "Are you a gift from God? You sure arrived at just the time I needed you." He sat back up and watched the action through his windshield, but his mind had drifted off.

He could bring her home. Company through the long, lonely evenings. Take her to work—Lana would love her. The community would adore her. The most popular dog around.

He saw one of the reporters setting up to interview someone straight ahead of him, but he wouldn't be able to hear anything. He grabbed his phone and went to the website advertised on the nearest van to search for a livestream.

Bingo. He clicked on it and listened while he watched the interview through his window.

"You are here for the prayer vigil tonight. Can you tell me why?" the reporter asked, angling the microphone toward the man.

"We are here to celebrate Isaiah Jackson's salvation. Regardless of the governor's decision, he now has a home in heaven! But we are also praying for God to have mercy and allow him more time to grow in his faith and do the Lord's work."

Jonas stopped the livestream. "Where was the mercy for the people he killed?" he said through clenched teeth. "Where is that young boy's chance to grow up and *do the Lord's work?*"

Kiki began to stir. She emerged from under the coat and shook herself. Her bright eyes went right to Jonas and her tail wagged.

He reached down between his legs under the seat, grabbed the mechanism to move it, and slid back. "Come on over."

She clambered over the center console, awkwardly landing on Jonas. He righted her, and she stood on his lap with her hind legs, her front legs on his chest. She dove for his face with her snout. He looked up laughing, dodging the pink tongue. Kiki was just as happy to bathe his neck and under his chin.

He stroked her bony body, urging her to sit still. "I think you should come home with me. We could be a team." After a bit, she wasn't settling, so Jonas retrieved the styrofoam container from the floor and poured some water from his water bottle. Kiki lapped up a few tonguefuls but lost interest quickly. She began to whine and prance, her puppy nails digging into his thighs.

Jonas realized she needed to pee. He glanced into the back seat and thought about what might be in the trunk. He had nothing to act as a leash, and she wasn't wearing a collar. He looked outside—he had backed into a parking space at the edge of the lot with a grassy verge behind the car.

"The grass is just a few feet away. You promise to stay

right beside me, we'll go for a quick walk?" She promised, her whole butt wiggling. He turned off the car and tossed the keys in the cupholder. Tucking her under one arm, he grabbed his coat, and stepped out of the car. At the edge of the grass, he set her down, watching her carefully to make sure she wouldn't run. Kiki had her nose to the ground wandering in circles like she was following the trail of a drunken rabbit.

Jonas put on his coat and relaxed. He looked up at the sky —any stars in the cold, clear night were washed out in the powerful spotlights around the prison walls. He walked slowly, Kiki glued to his side as she continued to sniff the ground.

Eventually, she found the exact right spot, and squatted. Jonas turned away, giving her space. The prayer vigil was maybe fifty yards away. He could hear singing now—faint, he recognized it as "Amazing Grace."

Someone from the group separated and turned, waving at Jonas. It was Michael. He and Kiki could walk over. Stretch their legs. He'd make an appearance and then be done with it.

Kiki circled Jonas's feet, dragging his attention back to her.

"Let's go, girl," he said. "Quick visit and then back to the warm car. Stay close." As he walked, she was underfoot, nearly tripping him. She wasn't letting him out of her sight.

He stopped a few yards from the prayer vigil, and Kiki plopped down between his feet. The folks were on the last verse.

"When we've been there ten thousand years
Bright shining as the sun,
We've no less days to sing God's praise
Than when we've first begun."

The hymn was one of Jonas's favorites, but the last verse especially made his throat tight and his eyes burn.

As the voices faded with the final notes, Michael began to speak to the group. "Let's pray. Lord, the words of this song remind us of your grace, and what eternity in your presence will be like. We thank you that—regardless of tonight's outcome—Isaiah Jackson's soul is safe with you. His name is engraved on the palms of your hands. He'll sing your praises for ten thousand years, and then start over again—"

Jonas stared straight ahead. He could not bow his head. He could not thank God for this. Anger flushed through him in a powerful torrent as he pictured his eternity—singing praises to the Lord with Kristy and Tyler and...Isaiah. He wanted to vomit.

"—we thank you for working through your servant, Jonas, to be the messenger of hope and grace and salvation for Isaiah and all the others on death row who have repented and turned their lives over to you—"

Jonas turned to leave. He was being credited as God's messenger of hope. A lie. He was the messenger of Jackson's destruction.

A commotion caught his attention. From the other side of the parking lot, past the media vans, a small group marched toward them. Their jaunty walking and sign-waving seemed aggressive. Jonas looked back at the prayer group—all heads were bowed, oblivious, as Michael droned on.

Jonas hissed, "Michael!"

Michael paused and looked at Jonas.

The protest group closed the gap—seeing their prey completely unaware—and when practically on top of them, began shouting and jeering. Anger and self-righteousness clashed with peaceful worship.

Someone sounded an air horn that ripped through the night. Jonas clapped his hands over his ears.

The media, smelling blood in the water, hustled toward them with cameras and equipment clattering behind.

Jonas was done.

He looked down. Kiki wasn't there.

Spinning in a circle, he scanned the parking lot. He spotted her, tail tucked and legs a blur, crossing the grassy verge past his car.

Jonas ran, calling her name.

Kiki didn't pause. She was almost to the prison access road.

Jonas saw a car approaching from the opposite direction on the main road, its headlights cutting the darkness. The turn signal blinked on. "KIKI!" Jonas ran as hard as he could, leaping onto the grass. He was too far away.

Kiki darted into the road just as the approaching car turned onto it.

The driver never saw her.

She ran across the white center line. The car hit her. Her small, thin body flew through the air. Bounced once. Landed on the far shoulder, in the ditch. The car kept going, never slowing.

Jonas sprinted across the road, still screaming her name, and stumbled down the side of the ditch where he'd seen Kiki disappear.

He stopped.

Kiki's broken body lay still. Twisted. Her eyes open, staring, gone. Blood trickled from her mouth—the only movement.

Jonas fell to his knees. He placed his hand on her crumpled rib cage, begging God for a heartbeat.

Distantly, he heard the commotion of the dust-up between protesters and pray-ers. Above him, he heard the sodium lamp buzzing. He vaguely thought someone was calling his name. He felt dampness soaking into the knees of his pants. Warm. Sticky.

But Kiki's heart was silent.

He fell forward. "No, no, no, please no," he sobbed into her shattered body. "GOD, no!"

CHAPTER TWENTY

JONAS DIDN'T KNOW how long he knelt there in the ditch, Kiki's body growing cold under his hands. Maybe seconds. Maybe hours. Time had stopped meaning anything.

His knees pressed into damp earth. Voices drifted from the parking lot above—shouting, engines, chaos continuing without him. Someone walked past on the shoulder, footsteps slowing, then hurrying on. He couldn't stay here.

He took off his coat and wrapped her in it. Standing, he cradled her broken body against his chest. Walked back to his car, moving like a ghost past the vigil's edges. No one stopped him.

He laid her in the back seat, still wrapped in his coat. Her blood had soaked through his shirt.

Jonas pulled onto the highway. Anger radiated from him in hot torrents. Grief fell on him in cold waves. He hunched over his steering wheel, shaking, as if he were trying to throttle it.

Within a mile or two, Jonas realized he was in no condition to drive. He signaled at the next exit and got off the highway. The diner from earlier was ahead of him. He'd pull in there and wait in the car until he was safe to drive home.

He parked by the dumpster, front facing in this time, with the headlights shining on the spot where he'd first seen Kiki scrounging for food. He threw the car in park. And just stared.

Fresh tears flowed down Jonas's face. He had rescued her from eventual starvation, and then he'd killed her. If he hadn't taken her, she'd still be here.

A tap on the passenger window startled him. Michael peered in, motioning for him to unlock the door. Jonas hit the unlock, and Michael opened the door. The overhead light came on as Michael got in. He glanced into the back seat—saw the coat-wrapped bundle—and nodded slightly. He closed the door.

"Talk to me, Jonas."

"How did you find me?"

"I followed you. I couldn't catch up to you before you left—what a mess with the chaos at the prison—so I jumped in my car to go after you. I'm really glad you decided to pull off the road."

Jonas stared at the spot in his headlights where he met Kiki. He could see that cute rump and wagging tail as it disappeared behind the dumpster.

"What happened, Jonas?"

"I found her right here. I fell in love with her. I thought she was a gift from God. I named her Kiki—" His voice broke. "He killed her."

"Let's go inside and talk." Michael motioned to the diner. "Get you cleaned up. Some coffee."

"I can't go in there. I'm a mess."

"It'll be fine. It doesn't look like anyone else is in there right now."

Jonas looked toward the diner. It was lined with windows, brightly lit from within. It did look empty. He held up his hands—they were coated in dried blood.

"Come on," Michael said, and opened the car door.

Jonas turned off the car and got out. They walked in silence to the front door. The cold bit through Jonas's shirt, but he didn't feel it. Michael opened the door for him and pointed to the bathrooms. Jonas headed that way on wooden legs.

After scrubbing his hands and splashing water on his face, then wiping it dry with scratchy brown paper towels, Jonas came out and joined Michael at a booth. Two coffees had already been set down.

They sat in silence, hands wrapped around the mugs. Jonas stared at the rising steam from his coffee.

"Michael, why did God kill her? Destroy my comfort?"

Michael was quiet for a long moment. "I saw what happened. I'm sorry about Kiki. I can tell you loved her."

Jonas's throat tightened. He couldn't speak. He nodded once—acknowledgement, not agreement.

"Is it right for you to be angry at God for this?" Michael asked quietly.

"Yes, it is." The rage built again, hot and sharp. "It was cruel. I wish it had been me hit by that car."

Michael nodded slowly. "You loved that dog. Met her two

hours ago, and you're ready to die in her place. That's real. That's good."

He paused. Pulled out his phone, scrolled for a moment, then looked back at Jonas.

"Can I read you something?"

Jonas said nothing. Michael took that as permission.

He read quietly: "'You pity the plant, for which you did not labor, nor did you make it grow, which came into being in a night and perished in a night. And should not I pity Nineveh, that great city, in which there are more than 120,000 persons...?'"

He looked at Jonas. Said nothing.

Jonas's coffee had gone cold. Outside the window, his car sat in the parking lot, Kiki's body still in the back seat.

Jonas stood. Turned. Walked out of the diner.

Into the night.

ABOUT THE AUTHOR

J. S. Helms is the pen name of Julie Helms, a wife, mother of two grown daughters, and—most recently—a grandmother. Over the years, she has been a sheep breeder, homeschool mom, curriculum store owner, and Bible study teacher.

She writes fiction that explores biblical themes through story rather than explanation, seeking to make complex theological ideas more tangible and human.

In addition to *The White Line*, she is the author of *Gods They Had Never Known*, a novel that draws on Genesis 6 and the Book of the Watchers. Releasing January 2027.

Find her short fiction at substack.com/@juliehelms2.

Contact Julie via PACEbooks@live.com.

VELLICHOR AND MORE

BOOKS AND ART THAT STIR THE SOUL AND INSPIRE THE DREAMER WITHIN.

www.ingramcontent.com/pod-product-compliance
Lightning Source LLC
LaVergne TN
LVHW091005080826
845145LV00003B/1129

* 9 7 8 1 9 6 2 8 9 1 0 8 0 *